John Day

A biographic memorial of Luther Colby

John Day

A biographic memorial of Luther Colby

ISBN/EAN: 9783337127190

Printed in Europe, USA, Canada, Australia, Japan

Cover: Foto ©Raphael Reischuk / pixelio.de

More available books at **www.hansebooks.com**

LUTHER COLBY.

A

BIOGRAPHIC MEMORIAL

OF

LUTHER COLBY

(FOUNDER OF THE BANNER OF LIGHT)

BY

JOHN W. DAY

> " *Thy voice comes down the rolling years*
> *Like ring of steel on steel !*
> *With it I hear the tramp of steeds,*
> *And the trumpet's silver peal !*
>
> " *But were the fainting to be raised,*
> *The sorrowing comforted, —*
> *The warrior vanished, and men saw*
> *An Angel stand instead !*"

BOSTON, MASS.
BANNER OF LIGHT PUBLISHING CO.
No. 9 BOSWORTH STREET
1895

ELECTROTYPED AND PRINTED BY

S. J. PARKHILL & CO.,

BOSTON.

DEDICATION.

To Mr. Isaac B. Rich, *the earnest friend and faithful co-partner of Mr. Colby for many years;*

To the Pioneers of Modern Spiritualism, *a hardy race, now passing rapidly to their well-merited "guerdon in the skies";*

And to the Youth of the New Dispensation, *who are reaping in joy what their forbears have sown in tears, and whose faces are now set toward the sunlight of world-wide victory:*

These Pages,

Briefly descriptive of an earnest and practical life now closed in the mortal, are lovingly dedicated.

J. W. D.

PREFACE.

THE writer of this unpretentious Memorial was closely associated with LUTHER COLBY in various capacities — as apprentice, compositor, reporter and assistant editor — from the very foundation (save one month) of the *Banner of Light*. While the partial failure of his eyesight — which necessitated sea voyages — and the Civil War demanded his attention from 1859 to nearly 1867, he was nevertheless constantly in touch with the establishment.

He was chosen by MR. COLBY, in 1872, to write the biography of Mrs. J. H. Conant, the first medium for *The Banner's* public circles; was trusted by him in all ways; and feels that he has been privileged to view the veteran editor in every light. These facts seem to be his best apology for presenting this volume, which has for its purpose a simple narrative of events transpiring, rather than any attempt at ornate display of language, — for which duty he was testamentarily appointed by his chief.

He herewith offers a simple tribute of respectful
remembrance to MR. COLBY, whom Spirit "Ouina,"
through the mediumship of Mrs. Cora L. V. Richmond, has truthfully characterized as an "impulsive,
turbulent, impetuous, childlike, generous, loving and
noble heart."

THE DEDICATION OF THE BANNER.

[The writer of this volume has in the following poem constructed a paraphrase of " Pulaski's Banner," which fifty years ago was a favorite among the schoolboy declaimers. He has been led to do so by an incident in the early history of the *Banner of Light*, which it is intended to illustrate. When the project of establishing *The Banner* was yet taking form in the minds of Mr. Colby and Mr. Berry, at a seance at which both were present, a spirit through the medium said that a determined leader would be necessary for the purpose in hand! Mr. Colby at once replied, in effect, that he would serve the spirit world in such capacity if desired, and his brave declaration was at once greeted with the high approbation of the unseen intelligence.]

WHEN New Truth with morning ray
Paled to Massachusetts Bay, —
Shed its broad'ning splendor down
On old Trimount's three-hilled crown,
Where the angels' censer swung, —
There, before their altar, hung
New-wrought banner that with prayer
Had been consecrated there.
And the spirit-hymn was heard the while,
Breathed down through a dim, mysterious aisle :

"Take thy banner! May it wave
Proudly o'er the good and brave
When the battle's distant wail
Breaks the slumber of earth's vale ;
When the clarion's music thrills
To the heart of human ills ;
When the land in conflict shakes,
And each strong creed, shivering, breaks.

"Take thy banner! and beneath
The war-cloud's encircling wreath
Guard — till human souls are free!
Guard it — God will prosper thee!

In the dark and trying hour,
In the sweep of dogma's power,
In the rush of blinded men,
His right arm shall guide thee, then!

.   .   .   .   .   .

"Take thy banner! and if e'er
Thou shouldst press a soldier's bier,
And the muffled drum should beat
To the tread of mournful feet,
Let this heaven-blest banner be
Martial cloak and shroud for thee." —

"AND THE WARRIOR TOOK THAT BANNER PROUD,
AND IT WAS HIS MARTIAL CLOAK AND SHROUD!"

INDEX.

———•———

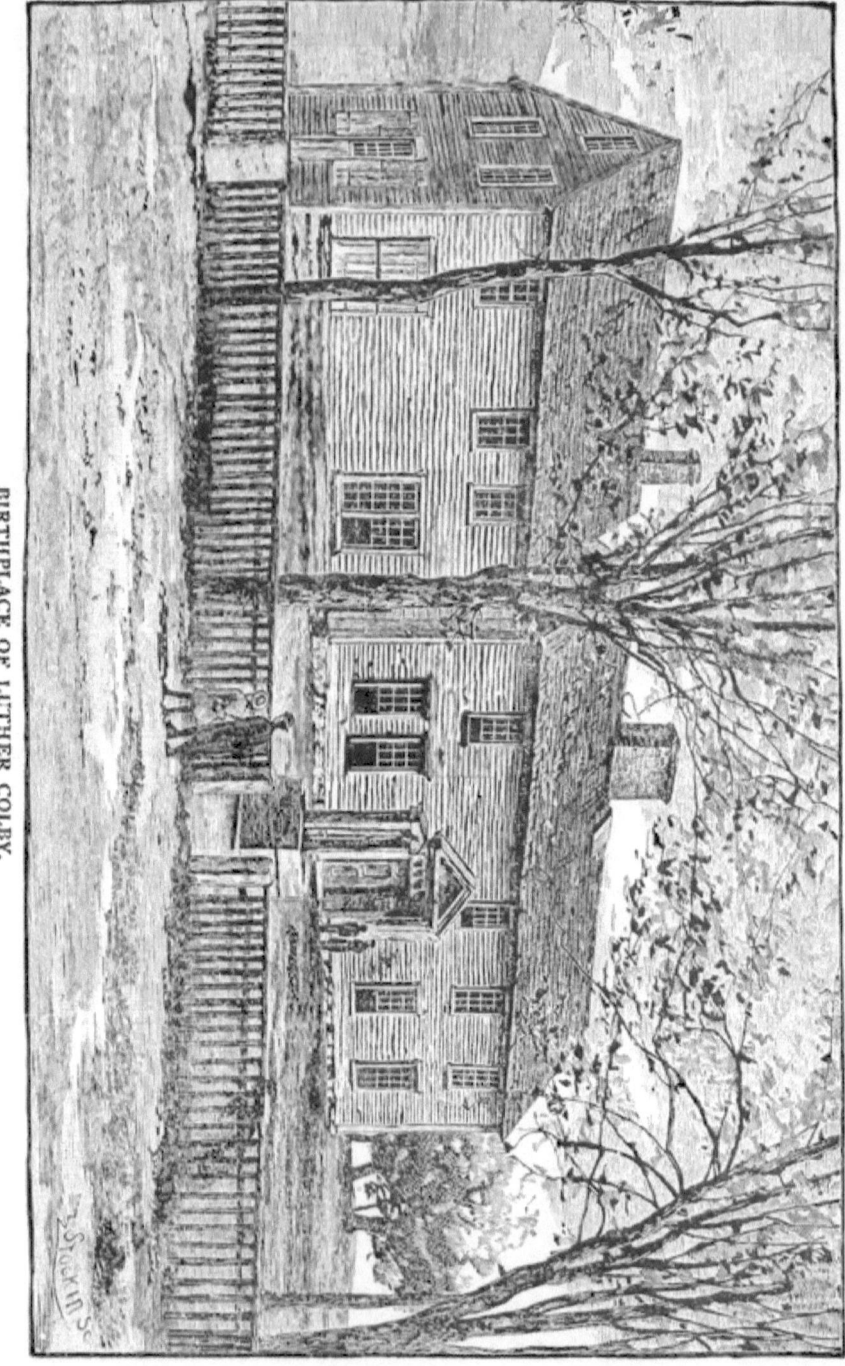

BIRTHPLACE OF LUTHER COLBY.

BIOGRAPHIC MEMORIAL OF LUTHER COLBY.

CHAPTER I.

"A MAN—CHILD IS BORN."

> "Our birth is but a sleep and a forgetting !
> The soul that riseth in us —our life's star—
> Hath had elsewhere its setting,
> And cometh from afar!"

SOME time on the 12th of October, 1814, the inhabitants of the then quiet town of Amesbury, Mass., said one to another, "A son is born to CAPTAIN WILLIAM and MRS. MARY COLBY."

It was an ordinary statement to make in the history of the large-familied New England of the early time ; and the narrowest bigot of the neighborhood — in equal consonance with the most open-hearted onlooker upon human life as it then existed in that uneventful settlement and elsewhere — could have drawn no lesson from the event, or sensed in any manner the grand prophecy which was involved in the coming of the infant stranger, who then once more, as he firmly believed, and always declared to the end of his mortal career, took upon himself the gradually increasing weight of mental care and physical expression which characterize this earthly state, and which his spirit had laid down in a previous and widely-different existence.

MR. COLBY was born in one of the old-fashioned dwellings peculiar to our staid ancestors. A picture of this edifice is given on an adjoining page.

The writer has the story direct from MR. COLBY's lips that his mother desired to name him "Martin Luther," but that his father, with a seaman's bluntness, thought that one given name was enough for a man to use as a "hailing word"; therefore the "Martin" was sacrificed, and the plain "Luther" became in this instance again historical.

MRS. MARY COLBY (MOTHER OF LUTHER COLBY).
Taken at the age of eighty-three years.

His mother long survived her husband, and lived to the remarkable age of eighty-seven; during her closing years she leaned with loving trust on the generous support of her devoted son.

At the time LUTHER COLBY set forth consciously upon his new round of mortal pilgrimage the theological world was as narrow, flat and circumscribed as was the physical world

Genesaically proclaimed with so much unction. The popularly accepted creeds set forth an irresponsible Oriental ruler who had been somehow ideally enthroned in the skies; the utter worthlessness of "works" — that is, a correct moral life — was held to by the pastors who pointed with proper partisan emphasis to the transcendent importance of a publicly-expressed faith in trinitarian speculations; and the acceptance of such beliefs was held by them as the only escape from "eternal fire." The chill doctrines of "predestination," "election," and "infant damnation" weighed like lead upon the hearts of men — though even then the sky of Faith was growing gray with a light which men called Unitarianism and Universalism — forerunner of the coming morn of Knowledge.

How wonderful then, by contrast with the present, the work accomplished for human welfare by the great Cause for the advancement of which Mr. Colby devoted his life-long labors! Ere his death in the mortal he saw the liberalizing process so ramifying among the Evangelical churches that save when called upon to "settle" ministerial candidates, or appoint foreign missionaries, their heart-wringing creeds are virtually abandoned as to utterance in the pulpits in the land.

The modern traveller who on some pleasant day walks the streets of old Plymouth, Mass., and revels in the beauteous vision of green trees and pleasant homes — the wide stretches of silver sand, the fresh ribbon of blue that old Ocean ever draws around the marine front of this historic town — can form but slight conception of that hour when upon a barren shore, amid the blasts of December and the rush of ice-laden waves, a little band of men and women instinct with the pursuit of what to them was a fact divine, landed in the face of unknown foes, and among (to them) unproved conditions of existence, bearing in their chilled and weary and yet resolute hands the hope of a great nation yet to be, and in their hearts, as did the Jews of old in the midst of their marching column, the Ark of the Covenant of that great continual Promise to the world : "The Truth shall make you Free ! "

The same traveller on now ascending the wind-swept hill whereon the first fort-church was erected (and another near by), will find inscribed on tombstone and monument the names of those who, in the mortal, dared the wintry deep for the freedom of conscience and the soul, but whose ascending spirits at last crossed the Atlantic of death to the brighter experiences of a Higher Life all undreamed of in their inmost conceptions ! Our nation delights to do them honor ! And in coming years, of a surety, the race of mankind, freed by Spiritualism's brave pioneers from the terror of the grave, shall give its soulful gratitude to the few who made known to the world by voice, pen and mediumship, the modern revelation of 1848 — the *demonstration*, rather, that "There is no death." Such pioneers were called on unquestioningly to give up position, popularity, even in many localities the common respect of their creed-blinded neighbors, that they might foster among men that with which the excarnated ones from the Beyond had entrusted them. Chief among those pioneers, while Spiritualism shall have existence among men, will be remembered the name of LUTHER COLBY

The infant COLBY grew to boyhood, developing gradually into vigorous strength and widening mental power. His early advantages for education — which were those pertaining to the common schools of the period — were fully improved ; and he finally took a step forward, associating himself with the "art preservative "; entering that grandest of schools, a printing-office, from which have graduated some of the foremost intellects of their times. He commenced at the age of fifteen his business career, as an apprentice at Exeter, N. H.

As if to practically acquaint him with the ground over which he must travel, and meet the inevitable attacks in after years of those who made of the Bible an inerrant and unquestioned fetich, his first important work as a printer was the

" setting up," with the aid of a fellow-apprentice, of an edition of " Scott's Family Bible " and the New Testament.

Some years were spent in fitting himself for the proper discharge of his duty in what he then considered his chosen avocation in life ; soon after attaining his majority he removed to Boston (1836) and was attached to the *Post*, one of the leading daily papers there, where he remained for some twenty years, passing, during that period, through every grade, from the composing to the editorial room. He then left the *Post* for a season of rest from his arduous labors — as he then thought — but really in fulfilment of plans which the world of spirits had concerning him.

CHAPTER II.

"Dwell no longer in the shadow
  Where the tomb-walls close around;
Rise! and twine your wreaths of welcome,
  For your 'dead,' your 'lost' are found!"
  —*Spirit* "*Metoka,*" *through Mrs. Conant's mediumship.*

UP to this time MR. COLBY had felt little interest as to a future existence. The bent of his mind led him naturally to the materialistic side ; and totally unable, as he was, to hold mental companionship with the dark views which the theology of his time inculcated, he instinctively gave in his adhesion to what was then called in the community by the broad and generic name of " infidelity " — then considered by the average easy-going citizen to be the most terrible of all offences against common morality and sound government. He thought, in view of the one-sided ideas of the churchmen, that the night of oblivion was a proper surcease of earthly sorrow, and became a stanch friend of Mr. J. P. Mendum, the veteran publisher of the *Boston Investigator*, with whom he was once a fellow-apprentice ; the friendship they established in early life existed between them as long as they both continued in the physical form.

He was also a bosom friend of the late Horace Seaver, the fearless editor of the *Investigator* for so many years. Both these old-time friends passed on from the mortal stage before him. He was also a pronounced friend and admirer of Rev. Abner Kneeland when that gentleman was prosecuted in Boston for alleged " blasphemy," in criticising the then popular conception of the deity.

MR. COLBY's rugged independence of thought, and utter freedom from all theological taint, fitted his mind, like rich virgin soil, to receive the seed of a new revelation which angel-workers were about to sow broadcast upon the earth. By personal investigation he became convinced of the conscious continuity of human life beyond the grave, and the power of the excarnated ones to intelligently make their presence known — under certain proper but imperative conditions — to the dwellers in the mortal form. *He was brought to recognize the soul within him;* he awoke to the consciousness of a broader life, and taking the sword and buckler proffered by the spirit armor-bearers, went grandly forth to conquer!

There is no need in a volume of this character to recount the story of the "Rochester Rappings" of 1848. Truth was again born in a manger; the glorious light of proven immortality streamed out upon the world from beneath the lowly roof and the sentinel poplar of Hydesville. Methodism (to change the metaphor) — which was itself primarily the result of spirit-working upon ministry and people, had become stranded on the shoal of popularity — had denied and lost "the power" which wrought so mightily with and upon the early men of that faith; and certain spirit intelligences appear to have decided to put off from the immovable ship and try to reach the heart of modern humanity in the life-boat of the Fox family, whose heads, paternal and maternal, were ardent disciples of the Wesleyan system.

From that early beginning the truth made rapid progress everywhere — and none too soon, when beneath the blows of materialistic doubt, the sneering reports of the learned medical dissectors of "the human form divine," and the palsying influence of a spiritually-dead clergy, the *hope* even of immortality was passing from the world! Investigators multiplied rapidly; among the earliest in Massachusetts, at least, were Dr. Henry F. Gardner, Rev. Allen Putnam, Mr. and Mrs. John S. Adams, Deacon Potter, Mr. and Mrs. A. E. Newton,

William Berry, Daniel and Mrs. Frances Farrar, Phineas E. Gay, and others. Through Mr. Berry's influence, Mr. COLBY was induced to be present at a Spiritual seance. His initial

PRESENT CONDITION OF THE FOX COTTAGE.

circle took place in 1856, in November, at the residence of Mrs. Stearns, on Cambridge Street (West End), Boston. There he first met Mrs. J. H. Conant (afterward the medium through whom *The Banner* Public Free Circles were inaugurated). He was at once attracted by her remarkable gifts, and strongly recommended her to the attention of Mr. Berry, who subsequently secured Mrs. Conant as the medium for a series of seances at his residence in North Cambridge, Mass. The most remarkable manifestations of spirit power, made alike on the physical and mental planes of demonstration, occurred at these meetings, which were held weekly.

If MARY COLBY was the earthly mother of the investigating LUTHER, Mrs. J. H. Conant speedily proved the maternal ancestor of his spirit-consciousness — since by the revelations given through her organism at these seances he was convinced — abandoning his bold agnosticism regarding the future of man, and taking fast hold on the truth that now appealed to his newly-recognized soul as a revelation from beyond the river of death!

CHAPTER III.

"Then-up with Truth's Banner—
  Let Vict'ry's winds fan her;
  She has borne her bright message
    To earth's every shore!
  In peace we'll attend her —
  In battle defend her
  With heart and with hand
    Like our fathers of yore."

MR. BERRY was told in the winter of 1856 that he would soon change his business, publish a paper to be called the *Banner of Light*, in the interests of the New Revelation, and be associated with MR. COLBY and others in its conduct, — all these predictions, made through Mrs. Conant's mediumship by invisible intelligences, proving historically true.

The object of *The Banner's* establishment was thus clearly set forth in its prospectus :

The spiritual manifestations now being developed demand a vehicle of communication which all will respect; and the faster good organs are multiplied, the better will it be for man and truth. While the world has sheets innumerable wherein are advocated the perishing interests of Time, it is important, nay, indispensable, that Truth should have its journals also — equal in point of mental and typographical merit to any — which plead and set forth the demands and developments of Eternity. . . . The *Banner of Light* has not been started without careful thought and preparation. It is in obedience to voices, nay, commands from on high, that its publication has been determined upon ; and every confidence is felt that great support will be extended, from regions of Light, to render it an instrument of good to man. *We know that this must be the case, for the evidence presented admits of no doubt or question.* In obedience, therefore, to a company on high, the *Banner of Light* is to be unfurled.

The first issue of *The Banner* was brought out at No. 17 Washington Street (old number), April 11, 1857, by a firm bearing the title "LUTHER COLBY & CO." It will be seen that the promises made to the original publishers by their invisible prompters were fully kept.

MR. COLBY, from the time of taking up the duty laid down by the spirit counsellors was, till his passage to the Higher Life, indefatigable in its every discharge.

The Banner's chief effort has always been to emphasize the fact that the mission of Modern Spiritualism is not the organization of a new sect, nor the special separation of its believers from the rest of the world by party lines, but rather to furnish a spiritual solvent, in which the existing forms of eschatological thought are to be saturated, illumination taking the place of gloom as the result. To the harmonious outworking of this early ideal MR. COLBY ever directed his energies. In the early days of the spiritual movement he was called upon for the sake and in defence of the Cause, to withstand alike the attacks of the bigoted clergymen, and the gibes of sceptical laymen ; even Harvard College itself did not shrink from attempting (though vainly) the task of shutting out the new light ; but he remained firm, in the face of most trying conditions, and with the support of his spiritual coadjutors, continued at all times true to his colors.

The history of the *Banner of Light* as a bold, honest and unselfish advocate of spirit-return and communion is before the world, and can speak always for itself. Since its inauguration it has found its way all over the globe wherever the English language is known. It has experienced the usual vicissitudes incident to business life. Its original firm of publishers changed in time to BERRY, COLBY & CO. ; at the period of the civil war the financial condition of the nation, generally, found its counterpart in that of this paper. *The Banner* was then issued at No. 3 1-2 Brattle Street, but business straits drove its publishers into a failure, which necessitated going through bankruptcy. Mr. Berry, after some preliminary movements, embarked on the sanguinary flood of the civil conflict, became an officer in a Salem, Mass., contingent, and fell, bravely fighting at the head of his command, at the battle of Antietam, Md., September 17, 1862.

The paper was revived, as to publication, by the late William White (then State printer of Massachusetts), and under the firm name of William White & Co.— Messrs. Isaac B. Rich, Luther Colby and Charles H. Crowell being co-partners — was continued at 158 Washington Street (old number).

The great and historic fire of 1872, which wrought such widespread destruction in Boston, burned the Parker Building, 158 Washington Street, where *The Banner* was located ; and but little was left to its publishers out of the ruin save a reduced insurance, the name of the paper, and their established mercantile reputation.

Some idea of the extent of this disaster to the publishers may be gained by the following extract from the "Report of the Boston *Banner* Relief Committee" issued November 23, 1872 :

Consulting with the proprietors of *The Banner*, we learn that their loss has been as follows :

Value of books burned, lowest wholesale price	$26,000
Loss of composing-room	3,500
Loss of mailing-machine, etc.	1,100
Loss of circle-room pictures, furniture, etc.	1,000
Loss of office furniture, safe, etc.	1,500
Subsequent loss by fire at Messrs. Rand, Avery & Co.'s establishment	2,000
Total,	$35,100

Amount of insurance, $20,000, of which probably thirty per cent., or $6,000 will eventually be obtained; leaving a net total loss of about $30,000.

This report was signed by H. F. Gardner, M.D., Chairman, Phineas E. Gay, George A. Bacon, Daniel Farrar, L. A.

Bigelow, Lizzie Doten, George W. Smith, Edward Haynes, Emma Hardinge-Britten, John Wetherbee, and others of the Music Hall Society.

The greatest sympathy (backed by pecuniary means) was aroused all over the country by the fate which had overtaken the paper ; and this feeling may be said to be crystallized in the following poem, published in the "*Banner of Light Appeal*" of November 26, 1872 :

OUR BANNER.

BY R. AUGUSTA WHITING.

Shall it not wave again ? — Banner of Light !
With record so glorious, with prospect so bright?
Oh ! shall it not rise from that smoldering pyre,
Where it sank overwhelmed by the demon of fire?

Shall it not wave again ? — Banner of Truth !
Consoling our aged ones, guarding our youth
From dangers that lurk 'neath the falsehood and guile
Of sirens that mock, and of tempters that smile ?

Shall it not wave again ? — Banner of Peace !
And love that is brotherly?   Say, shall it cease
Its angel-blest guidance and help to bestow
On the lone ones that wander in darkness below ?

Shall it not wave again ? — Banner of Joy !
That darkness and death have no power to destroy ;
That pointeth the mourner beyond the dark tide,
To the brightness in store on the ever-green side?

Shall it not wave again ? — Banner of Hope !
Still leading us onward with error to cope ;
To battle all tyranny, strong in the right,
That shall conquer at last in the struggle with might ?

Yes, it shall wave again !   Safe from the ire,
The wide-wasting wrath of the demon of fire,
Our Phœnix shall rise like a purified soul,
That through trial and triumph attains its heart's goal.

> Yes, it shall wave again !   Breezes more fair
> Than ever yet wafted its folds on the air
> Shall caress it. when, risen from ashes and flame,
> It shall shine like a gem on the breast-plate of fame.
>
> Again shall its " Light " re-illume the glad earth
> With bright rays of knowledge, with teachings of worth ;
> For the word has gone forth, over mountain and sea,
> Our " Banner " SHALL wave !   'Tis the will of the free !

Through the aid of generous friends and subscribers, the stricken firm at once set themselves at work to re-issue the paper, and took temporary headquarters at No: 14 Hanover Street.

On the 26th of April, 1873, Mr. William White suddenly passed to spirit life, at the age of sixty years — from heart-failure ; and the paper has since been brought out under the style of COLBY & RICH.

In the autumn of 1873 the publication office of *The Banner* was removed to No. 9 Bosworth Street (then Montgomery Place), a location which had been purchased and specially fitted up for the purpose by its business manager, Isaac B. Rich.   From this place it still continues to make its appearance regularly.

CHAPTER IV.

MR. COLBY'S MEDIUMSHIP.

"Alas! faint hearts, who are longing ever
  On the lofty mountain tops to stand,
Instead of making a brave endeavor
  To climb the hills that are close at hand :
If we brighten one life that had else been dreary,
  If we help one soul to be strong and true ;
Our hearts may sing though our feet be weary,
  We are doing the work that is ours to do."
— *The Indian Helper.*

MR. COLBY was, from the first, aided in his labors by un-seen powers. He was — and willingly acknowledged it — in an especial sense cared for by the Invisible Workers in the Higher Life, and was himself endowed with a mediumship — involving the clairvoyant, impressional and automatic writing phases — which as to its results often called out the wonder and astonishment of his friends and co-workers in the mortal.

The present writer is cognizant of many instances in proof of this assertion, one of the most direct being the following : The Rev. Allen Putnam (now ascended to the reward of a brave and useful life on earth) and myself were one day present in *The Banner* editorial rooms, considering with MR. COLBY some matter bearing on the Cause ; the visit being at an end, he (Putnam) started to go from the room ; when he had reached the door, MR. COLBY suddenly called upon him to stop, adding, "Your spirit friends wish you to sell [certain railroad stocks, which he named] at once." Mr. Putnam, who, perhaps by reason of its suddenness, did not attach sufficient faith to the warning, afterward told the writer and MR. COLBY, too, that had he acted on the injunction thus enunciated, he would have been greatly benefited financially.

Mr. Colby's mediumship often manifested itself in quaint and original impressions of men, things and events. It was also in obedience to its promptings, aided by those of Mrs. Conant, that the _Banner of Light_ Free Public Circles were undertaken at the National House, Boston, in the first year of the paper's existence. He, in obedience to the same promptings, formed that other agency of so great and extended usefulness, "The God's Poor Fund" of _The Banner_— aid from which in the past years has been extended to worthy parties all over this continent. In the same way he was led to establish the "Editor-at-Large" project, by which for several years money was raised whereby the late Prof. S. B. Brittan was secured to answer attacks made in the secular press on Spiritualism and its advocates. Through a like prompting he was led, in the second year of _The Banner's_ existence, to anticipate the modern custom of printing the full reports of sermons of popular divines in the columns of the weekly press outside that of their special denominational groups ; this plan he followed with the greatest success — the pastors selected being Rev. Henry Ward Beecher and Rev. E. H. Chapin of New York. He may be said to have been among the very first, if not the founder of this custom ; and as long as he was allowed the privilege of taking _verbatim_ the reports of these sermons, he proceeded to work up the circulation of _The Banner_ to a remarkable figure. The right, however, when it was discovered to have a market value, was taken from him (though for no alleged fault in these reports) and given to a religio-secular daily of Boston, then making great efforts to enlarge its edition.

The following sketch of Mr. Colby's nature, as psychometrically revealed, was made by that renowned medium, Mrs. C. M. Decker, of New York (afterward Mrs. J. R. Buchanan), at the request (so an indorsement found upon it states) of Charles R. Miller, on the 15th of September, 1879.

Mr. Miller, being on a visit to the lady regarding some independent *spirit* writings, asked her to examine a letter he had just received from MR. COLBY — though he did *not* inform her *who* was the author of the letter. Mr. Miller transcribed her reading *verbatim*, and sent it to MR. COLBY. He who was described and she who psychometrized have now both gone to the home of the spirit.

"'This is not a spirit [she had just been reading spirit-writing]. This man is largely spiritual. I feel a spiritual elevation. This person is developed in the region of the spiritual. I feel that this is a man ; a great amount of business talent ; a great amount of writing talent. I should think he was a journalist, or newspaper man ; he knows how to take care of himself. He is not to be thrust aside ; when he wants to say or do a thing he says and does it — a fearless character. He writes better than he talks ; he thinks rapidly, and writes better than he speaks. When he writes he is controlled by spirits, and is very mediumistic. This man has a great deal to do with people ; has a great many subjects and people to deal with ; he is well sustained, and has a great number of friends ; he works hard.

"'I think he is an American, but, at the same time, his writing, correspondence and work extend across the water, and to other countries ; his writings and labors are widely extended ; subjects from his paper are read and translated into other languages. There is a great deal of spiritual faith and trust in this man. He has an advanced female spirit around him that does a great deal of good ; he needs it, too.

"'If you know this man, he is a good friend — he is a good friend of yours. This man is not dictatorial in his writings, rather mild and genial ; he prefers not to mix up with the wrangle of life : he is sometimes drawn into it, but keeps as clear of it as he can ; he is a character that most people like to deal with, as he throws around them a spirit of geniality and confidence. Nothing grieves this man more than to make a retraction from any misstatement that may have been given him. He would be likely to scold a little about that, but he

has usually an equanimity of disposition.   There is very much
to the man ; he is not a politician in the common sense ; he
would like to see good government, and to contribute to it ;
but he is discriminating, and would not mix up with current
politics ; he would not use his pen in that direction.   No.

"'His character is one that does not decide hastily on any
question or problem that comes before him ; he would revolve
it in his mind and weigh it decidedly before publishing.   This
man as a publisher would consult all sources of information
before deciding.   He is exceedingly conscientious, and is a
great stickler for the truth ; he has not an enthusiastic nature
— more earnestness than enthusiasm in his nature.

"' Physically, I should say this person was stout, solidly
built.   I see a form as large or larger than you are, and a man
that would be likely to hold on to life for many years.   I don't
see any physical disarrangement, except a fulness about the
head and back base of brain.   This may result from over-
tasking the brain.

" ' To sum it all up, this is a grand and good spirit, and one
that is calculated to give and receive pleasure in this life.
There seems to me some approaching change connected with
him, but can't tell what it is.   I see a long avenue before me ;
on the road I see a great many stumps, broken branches and
ragged appearances, but on the other side is freshness and
uniformity, which I interpret as indications of success and
prosperity.' "

The medial outreaching from MR. COLBY to the sensitives
of the country brought to them oftentimes strength in trial —
and on repeated occasions a return tide of appreciation.
Among his papers (as an instance) the following letter was
found by the author of this memorial — bearing the endorsed
date of September 18, 1883.   Old Spiritualists on reading it
will recognize the name of Ed. S. Wheeler as that of a foremost champion of the Cause ; he was then *near* the mystic
line, beyond which he soon after passed to the brighter land.

ON THE BOUNDARY.

I am where I can look on both countries, and I see the business of both. Never! Never!! Never!!! doubt that you are guided and that you are cared for personally. The true intent and purpose may not always find its complete and perfect interpretation, but the master of the storm will succeed in directing the course, not only of your own life but of the great enterprise of which you have so long been a part. Tempest threatens, clouds darken, and in your great physical weakness you almost despair. Stand firm, this late hour; the elements of nature are in sympathy with your purpose and that of those in whose loving care you make your advance. Truth shall triumph; your guides shall screen you from every infernal thunderbolt. . . .

Whether I return, remain in the body and meet you again face to face, or pass within the veil to the land so inviting to the heart-sick and weary, remains equally probable; in either case, I am and shall be, as for so many years, in heart-felt sympathy,

Your sincere friend,

ED. S. WHEELER.

This feeling also found utterance in the following lines, in appreciation of his life services, by Mrs. Emma Tuttle (contributed to *The Banner* for November 5, 1892), which may be regarded as the concentred expression, by a spiritually-minded and prescient authoress, of the recognition of his services which after-years shall fully bring:

THE BANNER BEARER OF SPIRITUALISM.

TO LUTHER COLBY, ESQ., ON HIS BIRTHDAY.

His hair is white, his soul is white;
  Truth lights his earnest face.
Halt, crowding infantry! fall back,
  And give the veteran place.

Straight as a forest pine he stands,
  Meeting unflinchingly
The storms of winds or human minds,
  Rushing in madness by.

His ears are catching high commands,
  Outspoken from the skies;
His *Banner* gives them to the world
  To read, and thus grow wise.

Long may our veteran worker live,
  Our growing ranks to lead;
Long may our heads and hearts incline
  His strong commands to heed.

Berlin Heights, O.   EMMA ROOD TUTTLE.

In the same vein a prominent man among the old-time workers once wrote to him :

You are eminently a man of *heart;* your influence upon your readers through your paper is of far higher quality and more telling in its effects, as the predominating influence is a *germinal* one.   Your readers get your magnetism and it acts like spiritual leaven upon them; they become educated by absorption, no matter if their eyes do not take in your words; the old family feeling comes upon them when they open *The Banner.*

Concerning MR. COLBY'S mediumship, and the open and willing generosity with which he instantly yielded to his impressions, Dr. J. M. Peebles, of San Diego, Cal., known in all lands as " The Spiritual Pilgrim," thus testifies in a memorial letter written to *The Banner:*

" The real goodness of Brother Colby was not understood as it should have been by many Spiritualists," wrote Brother Moses Hull to me last week, adding, " When I was once in straitened financial circumstances he took from his purse fifty dollars and handed me, with the remark, '*Say nothing about it.*'   Now that he has passed up, on to the beautiful highlands of immortality, it can do no harm to mention it."
How vividly do I remember of once sitting by him when opening his morning pile of letters.   Sensing the invisible aura he would say, inspirationally and psychometrically, " This is a good woman and a good medium." " This man is always in trouble, and he seems to want to throw it on to me."   " This man is angry because I don't publish his long communication."   " This brother has half-a-dozen different controls, and is all mixed up.   He is a good-hearted man; I must write to him."   And so through the pile, without opening, would he read the spirit, if not the very wording of the letters.

Once, I remember, when annoyed by reported exposures and mediumistic idiosyncrasies, and exclaiming " These inharmonics will wear me out," he seized his pencil and wrote, automatically, these words: " The day succeeds the night, the spring the winter; all will be well in the end, Luther." He immediately brightened up, saying, " That's Berry; it sounds just like him." The same day I saw him hand a poor mediumistic woman a five-dollar gold piece; and in the afternoon, walking with him to the post-office, I saw him enclose a twenty-five-dollar post-office order to a poor struggling young medium in Michigan, Mr. ——. He is yet in the Spiritualist lecture field. And yet some Spiritualists wonder " why the *Banner of Light* is not rich!"

George A. Bacon, of Washington, D. C., a close friend of MR. COLBY for many years, bore witness as follows on this topic, in his memorial letter to *The Banner:*

Few, even of those who thought they knew him intimately, realized the glorious measure of his mediumship. Instead of seeking its display, he guarded it with almost sacred modesty. Scores of instances, extending over many years, occurring when least expected, and under every conceivable condition, are personally known to me, which if related would naturally bewilder the reader, so startling were many of these manifestations.

To illustrate his intense sensitiveness one instance will suffice. Quietly sitting with him one day in his editorial room, which was on the third floor, he suddenly arose from his desk, and began to stride up and down the room under great excitement, storming with angry feelings, to which he gave vent. Resuming his seat after awhile he calmly began writing again, when he turned and asked, " What does all this mean?" I replied, " Perhaps it will explain itself." In the course of a few minutes a rap at the door, and a visitor entered, which did solve the problem. This pseudo-friend was a chronic critic of microscopical characteristics, whose sense of his own personal importance filled the universe. Voluble, complaining, assertive, tiresome, he had called to relieve his fault-finding spirit, and the sensitive editor had unwittingly sensed the man's antagonism the instant he entered the office, ten minutes before he appeared upstairs.

No more consistent or truer friend to mediums ever wielded pen or raised a voice in behalf of these sensitives than this same sturdy man, who by gift of organization was a representative of this very class.

MR. COLBY was wont, on occasion, to "dash off" impromptu, sonnet-like productions, akin to the subjoined — sometimes

signing them " Digby," and at others with his name or initials.
They may be regarded as the cropping out of a poetic vein in
his nature which the circumstances of his career prevented a
following up to any extent :

ARS LONGA VITA BREVIS.

" Art is long and life is short,"
Is what Digby has been taught;
Now he strives with great endeavor
To prove that man doth live forever.
Here we stay a certain time,
Then pass to a finer clime —
Evidence of this appears
After unbelief of years —
Where each soul a home shall find
Smoothly suited to his mind.

DIGBY.

JE-HO-VAH.

Within the holy realm of deepest thought,
Where Wisdom's precepts are so fully taught,
Resides a Band of Oriental Seers,
Whose lives are measured by unnumbered years.
Here beauteous flowers of every form and hue
Glisten in brightness with the morning dew,
Emitting odors of such rare perfume
That keep them ever constantly in bloom.
This is the land Celestial — this the Throne
Which wafts its wisdom unto every zone ;
This, too, doth guide each planet in its course
From which the spheres derive their mighty force.
This is the Godhead ! — this the realm of law —
From which all Nature doth its incense draw :
This much I know ! — and, knowing, know no more !
And that is why JE-HO-VAH I adore.

LUTHER COLBY.

Mr. COLBY's mental characteristics, displayed by him to the
very close of his life in the mortal — his faith in the ultimate

triumph of the Cause, his determined combativeness in its
defence, his willingness to be guided at all times by the gentle
voices of the invisible ones speaking to his inner ear — may
be likened to those in the old Indian tale of "The Standard
Bearer" : It is related that an old elephant was engaged in a
battle on the plains of India. He carried on his back the
royal ensign, the rallying-point of the host. At the beginning
of the fight his driver was killed: he had given the elephant
the word to halt when he received the fatal wound. The
obedient beast stood still while the battle closed around him
and the standard he carried. He never stirred a foot, refusing
to advance or retire, as the conflict became hotter and fiercer,
until the Mahrattas, seeing the standard still flying steadily in
its place, refused to believe that they were beaten, and rallied
again and again round the colors.

All this while, amid the din of battle, the patient animal
stood straining its ears to catch the sound of that voice it
would never hear again. At length the tide of conquest left
the field deserted. The Mahrattas swept on in pursuit of the
foe, but the elephant stood immovable, with the ensign waving
in its place. No bribe or threat could move it from the position it had been ordered to occupy. They finally sent to a
distant village and brought the driver's little son. The noble
beast seemed then all at once to remember how the driver, his
master, had sometimes given his authority to the little one,
and immediately, with all the shattered trappings clanging as
he went, he paced quietly and slowly from the field of battle
under the guidance of a child!

CHAPTER V.

"GONE HOME."

" The rest that earth denied is thine ;
   Ah, is it rest, we ask,
Or, traced by knowledge more divine,
   Some larger, nobler task ?
Enough ; there is a world of love ;
   No more we ask to know ;
The hand will guide thy ways above
   That shaped thy task below!"

MR. COLBY, the veteran *Banner of Light* editor, as you know has crossed the peaceful river, and joined the multitude of the immortals. So pass my old compeers, one by one — JUDGE JOHN W. EDMONDS, ROBERT DALE OWEN, WILLIAM DENTON, A. E. NEWTON, S. B. BRITTAN, EPES SARGENT, HENRY KIDDLE, DR. CROWELL, and now LUTHER COLBY, mourned by thousands upon thousands of Spiritualists.— J. M. PEEBLES, in *London Medium and Daybreak.*

THE author of this Memorial wrote for and published in *The Banner* for October 13, 1894, a leading editorial titled as above, the significance of which, at least, he feels, pierced to the heart of every Spiritualist wherever the New Revelation has a name among men :

" It becomes the duty of *The Banner* to announce to its many readers in every civilized land beneath the sun, the demise of its Founder and Senior Editor, LUTHER COLBY.

" No announcement of his sickness has been made in these columns, because of the direct wish of the sufferer, who, till a short time before his passage from the mortal, had the hope that the power of will, and a naturally strong constitution, would once more place him on his feet among men. It is only just to state, however, that for nearly two years past MR.

COLBY has felt the depressing influence of age, and has been fain, perforce, to yield the larger portion of his former labors to younger hands. . . .

"The event which must come to all finally drew near ; and at five o'clock on the morning of Sunday, October 7th, just five days before the completion of his eightieth year, he entered Higher Life from the Crawford House, Scollay Square, Boston, which had been his home for some twelve years past.

"He was cared for during his last illness of nearly two months, by Mrs. W. P. Thaxter, of Boston (wife of Mr. W. P. Thaxter of the Crawford), who exhibited to the aged sufferer all the tender sympathy and loving care which a daughter could have displayed, though no blood relationship existed between them. We are sure that our readers — the elderly men and women, especially, who have followed MR. COLBY's work from the days of their youth — will feel to join with us in the expression of reverent thanks to this grand trance medium, who willingly closed her office and abandoned her own special work, to smooth the path of this wounded veteran soldier of the Truth toward 'the narrow way that leadeth to the Paradise of God.'

"MR. COLBY was never married. He leaves one brother, Moses L., who, with Mr. F. F. Morrill (son of his old friend, the late ex-Senator George W. Morrill, of Amesbury, Mass.), aided by his bedside.

" *The Banner's* leader (March 10, 1894) announcing the commencement of Volume LXXV, had this sturdy sentence, which its newly-arisen senior editor may now, by the prescient ear, be heard avowing to mortals from beyond the veil : 'The years hasten to the century's close. It matters little where or how we work, but work we assuredly shall, as a living inheritor of the great Kingdom of Truth, that is without end !' "

The announcement of the demise of MR. COLBY drew forth many appreciative tributes from the press of Boston — the *Globe, Journal, Advertiser, Post, Herald*, etc. Respectful and appreciative mention was also made concerning his transition by the Spiritualist and Reformatory press of England, the Continent, Australia and America.

The *Boston Daily Globe*, in the course of a lengthy editorial bearing upon his history and decease, said :

His form was erect to the last, though he bowed his head slightly as if in deep thought. His face was ruddy and his eye bright when last seen upon the street, about three months ago. . . .

He was in many ways a remarkable man. He remained at his editorial post until close to the last. It was always a desire of his that he should " die in harness." . . .

He was well known to all Spiritualists in Boston, and, of course, to thousands who came to visit this Mecca of Spiritualism, but he also came into contact with millions of Spiritualists through his paper, and by the large majority of these he was looked upon with reverence. . . . He lived in the realm of spiritual enfoldment. He believed that he was the message-bearer of the angels, or, as he would say, the instrument of the spirits. . . .

Under this inspiration he became the spiritual friend and teacher of thousands of men and women who only knew him through the *Banner of Light*. To many thousands of his readers, LUTHER COLBY was prophet and priest, and the utterances of *The Banner* were regarded as infallible.

One secret of MR. COLBY'S success as an editor was his reputation as an honest believer in Spiritualism and his adherence to what he felt to be the truth. In recent years his editorial labors were not so arduous as those of his early manhood, but the old pioneer spiritual paper has always borne the name of LUTHER COLBY as editor. . . .

He was a manly man, a laborious worker, charitable and generous, frank and open-hearted, a devoted son and a faithful friend.

The *Boston Daily Post*, with which his young manhood was so closely identified, bore this among other tributes to his memory :

Thoroughly honest in his personal belief in the phenomena of Spiritualism, he was able to exert an influence which has spread far and wide with marvellous results. His sincerity was unquestioned and undoubted. He had the respect of the public, the confidence of all with whom he was brought in contact. And his services in the cause of Spiritualism are recognized as those of an honest man, honestly striving for principle.

THE OBSEQUIES.

On Wednesday afternoon, October 10, 1894, the spacious auditorium of the First Spiritual Temple, erected by Mar-

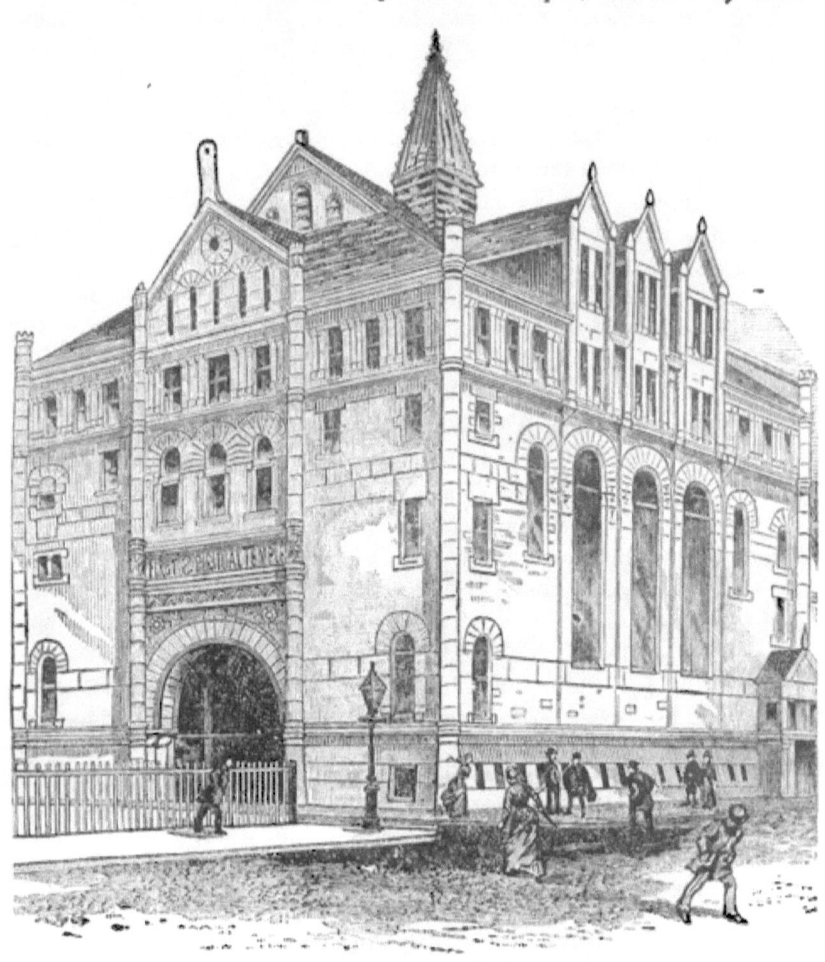

FIRST SPIRITUAL TEMPLE.

cellus S. Ayer, of Boston, at the corner of Exeter and Newbury Streets, was the scene of the funeral rites held in grateful remembrance of MR. COLBY'S work when in the mortal, and in respect to the physical tenement wherefrom his enfranchised spirit had arisen to the outworking of new demands upon its energies.

The Spiritual Fraternity Society, through Mr. Ayer, placed the Temple in the hands of the Committee of Arrangements; and a large assemblage of people, including representatives of nearly every form of religious belief or non-belief in the community, convened to join in the silent expression which their presence involved, that they had lost a friend, a helper, or one in whom their respect was strongly centred.

Moses L. Colby (the only surviving brother), and other relatives, were of the assemblage.

Among others in attendance were Isaac B. Rich, partner of the deceased, and Mrs. Rich; John W. Day, editor of the *Banner of Light*, an associate with MR. COLBY for the past twenty-seven years; Mr. F. F. Morrill, of Amesbury, son of his old friend, the late ex-Senator George W. Morrill; Charles McArthur of New York, a faithful co-worker for years; Mr. and Mrs. W. P. Thaxter; Mr. and Mrs. S. H. Bradley; Mr. Charles J. Rich; Mr. and Mrs. C. S. Mountford; Mrs. B. F. Smith, medium of *The Banner's* Message Department; Mr. and Mrs. William S. Butler; Charles G. Wood and wife; W. N. Eayrs, foreign translator for *The Banner;* Mrs. J. K. D. Conant; William Harris, manager of the Columbia Theatre; Mr. Simeon Snow; Mr. J. Frank Baxter; Mr. M. S. Ayer; Henry Goodwin, of the Crawford House, where for so many years MR. COLBY made his home; Charles W. Sullivan; Mrs. Sarah A. Byrnes; Mr. and Mrs. Benjamin Loring; Mrs. Carrie M. Sawyer; Mrs. Dr. Shaw; Mr. Alonzo Danforth; Mr. C. Frank Whittaker; Dr. J. A. Shelhamer; Dr. W. A. Towne; Mr. and Mrs. Lewis; Mrs. M. A. Wilkinson, President of Hollis Hall Society; Mrs. A. E. Barnes, of the Ladies' Aid Society; Professor and Mrs. Longley; Mr. and Mrs. Jones; L. L. Whitlock; and Mrs. Hattie Stafford-Stansbury.

The floral offerings made on the occasion were many in number, and elegant in character.

A voluntary by George H. Rider, organist of the Temple, opened the exercises, at 2.30 o'clock, after which Lyman C.

Howe, of Fredonia, N. Y., who was then speaking for the Society, offered an invocation.

Mrs. Hattie E. Dodge, the Temple's soloist, then rendered touchingly the Spiritual song: "Only a Thin Veil between Us."

Dr. H. B. Storer, the veteran Spiritualist speaker of Boston, then made introductory remarks, and delivered the address; his words being marked by deep feeling as to enunciation, and receiving the evident acceptance of responsive hearts:

ADDRESS BY DR. H. B. STORER.*

The old, old fashion of death has passed upon our friend, and the body that has served him well, having become at last an encumbrance, may be put away. Less enduring than the shadow of it cast by the camera upon the plate, it is the least valuable of all the spirit's possessions. We think of it as wonderfully made, passing all human skill or human knowledge, and yet destined at the last, as all mere instruments are destined, to pass away after its uses have been served. And therefore, concerning the body, it matters little how it shall be bestowed; if it be buried, as has been the custom for ages, beneath the soil, and there be dissolved into the elements by the process of decay, away from the sight of men, or whether it be dissolved more speedily by cremation, as was the wish of our friend, it shall be rendered at last into impalpable powder, and it is a matter of little concern what the process may be. It may be a matter of sentiment, with many it is a matter of choice; but whatever the disposition of the body may be, it is less than nothing as compared with the resurrection of the man himself from the encumbrances of the body. And therefore to-day, dear friends, if any of you feel like going down into the grave with the body, it is only because your mortality hugs you close; it is because you have not yet become accustomed to separate those thoughts of yourself from this garment you wear — from this body that serves your uses. It has been a clear perception of seers that so far as the outer garment was concerned, it is less than nothing as compared with the development of those interior graces that pertain to the spirit. How different the signification of this event in the public mind from that which prevailed fourscore years ago, when our friend was born. Then Death was the king of terrors; then the spirit-world was an undiscovered

---

* This address, which is given in full, appeared in the *Banner of Light* for October 20, 1894, as also did the other speeches which are here necessarily condensed.

country; then the condition of the soul was problematical, and in the absence of all knowledge, human speculation drew its pictures of the future life in the most sombre colors, because men took counsel of their fears rather than their hopes. Being imperfect themselves, they felt that the Being whom they professed to believe was the author of all good was himself capable of petty passions and the imperfections of our human nature, and therefore they could see nothing beyond the grave except the possibility of torture; perhaps, mercifully perhaps, annihilation; but they could not look up trustingly and see the Beauty of that Being, typified in the loveliness which we find in nature, and the affection which is manifested in so many forms. No, they had not attained that sweet confidence in the infinite goodness of God which we enjoy in these latter days. It was simply a belief that in meeting God they were to meet a great judge who was perfect; that with all their imperfections on their heads they were to meet a perfect Being. Under such circumstances who could do otherwise than to dread death? It was into such an atmosphere and into such a sphere of belief that our friend was born eighty years ago.

Fortunately, he does not seem as a boy to have inherited any tendency to superstition, to dogmatism and theological conceit. Marked out, as he undoubtedly was, for a career of usefulness, which is illustrated by his whole life, he was permitted to be unhindered by any such burden upon his spirit. He was of a genial nature, loved by his comrades and loving them. After leaving the public schools, where the rudiments of education were taught, he entered upon the study of that profession, if I may so call it, in which he engaged in after years. He entered the best college that exists among men, the printing office; because in the printing-office less care is given to the mere technical details of acquirement; it is not the memory that is cultivated only, but especially the printing-office develops a knowledge of events of human life, and every process of the compositor is a constant criticism, and he is steadily being educated upon the very sentences that he is putting in type. As they pass before him his mind discerns the imperfection, if there be such, and when a thought is felicitously expressed, some idea bursts upon him, and as he proceeds he enjoys fully whatever is presented; his mind enlarges, his sphere of thought increases, he is led to study and investigate. The printer and the editor are the best types to-day of educated men. And I say this, because I realize that our friend's education was not after the standard methods. He constantly rose in this profession from the time he first entered it, when he was fifteen years of age, until he came to the great city — came here to Boston as a compositor, and gradually rose to the editorial chair. In this process of education he had to deal with current events, to discriminate between the truthful and the false, to give attention to matters that pertain to human interests, to be familiar with many things; and therefore his education was broad; the tendency of his mind was to discard narrowness, and he was prepared to see things as they were and to judge righteous judgment. Now this preparation was all necessary in the work to which our friend was appointed; and when I affirm my conviction that our lives are planned and arranged in the minds of those who are to assist us in our work, I affirm what has been confirmed in the life of our friend, that those who are most truly spiritual believe that these events that occur in our daily lives are not merely the product of chance, the result of a combination of circumstances, but were ordered, and are a part of a perfect system that pervades the entire universe.

Our friend came at last incidentally to notice the reports of manifestations from the spirit-world, occurring somewhere, occurring in many places, cumulative, week after week, month after month, new statements of what occurred in different places, manifestations essentially similar, curious and mysterious at first, but of no spiritual concern. But his mind kindled to the subject, and he was led to investigate. In doing so he was fearless; he didn't apprehend any trouble from the censure of his friends; he didn't anticipate any adverse criticism. He entered upon the investigation as he had opportunity, and that investigation brought him to conviction that there is indeed communication between that sphere of light above and around us, the spiritual sphere and the mortal state here on earth. He came to perceive that to be a great truth that must revolutionize the thoughts and opinions of mankind, must touch every community, and must eventually make man better known to himself as a spiritual being than he ever has been able to know through his senses. Therefore, he at once proposed that there should be a paper started. First of all, it was to be a literary paper, and have a department in which Spiritualism should be represented. But the very first issue of that paper indicated the courage with which the work of presenting the truths of Spiritualism was to be carried forward. He said distinctly in the first editorial: " We shall not necessarily believe all that its advocates say, but we shall not refuse to listen to what may be said. We shall publish nothing that is not well authenticated as reports of phenomena." The record of the *Banner of Light* has been a record of the fidelity of its editor to the maintenance of the principles first enunciated. I wish you to feel that it is impossible for me to speak of LUTHER COLBY without speaking of the *Banner of Light.* It was wrapped about him; it was wrapped about his inmost soul; his whole soul went out in and through that paper to mankind, his purpose being to present and make clear the great revelation that he believed involved so much.

And I must say of my friend, that you may see him as he was, that he was a very courteous gentleman, almost a gentleman of the old school, a man of natural politeness, with suavity of manner, never boisterous, but stating calmly, firmly and distinctly what he had witnessed, and simply saying: " What I have witnessed you may witness. The indications from phenomena almost constitute a philosophy, that the world will come to understand, and by knowing will be the better for it." His work for these many years, since the first issue of that paper in 1857, has been continuous — in late years with the assistance of an associate editor ; and he has continued to perform his duties in the editorial chair, nearly all the matter that has been published passing under his surveillance. As I have said, he was true to this : Articles that could not present evidence of the phenomena narrated were set aside, and those sentiments that were not in harmony with the fundamental principles of Spiritualism were set aside. *The Banner* has been cautious, conservative, bold, courteous, distinct, and never has been subservient to anything but the right, never could be prevented from uttering its best thought, and it is that which has secured for it the continued approval and appreciation of the people ; and wherever it has gone — and it has gone all over the world — the name of LUTHER COLBY, a personal stranger to the multitude who associated it with the *Banner of Light*, has been a synonym of that devotion which he ever manifested to the truth, and that firmness of conviction which from the first he felt in the revelations of Modern Spiritualism.

Oh, dear friends, could I gather all the tributes from loving hearts all over this world to the memory of LUTHER COLBY ; could I gather the tributes from those who have been educated in the Spiritual Philosophy, largely through the instrumentality of himself, the tributes of hundreds and thousands of hearts that have been warmed and quickened by his influence and which have come into welcome association with the higher life — what a wealth of appreciation of his labors would this indicate ; not because he was altogether a perfect man, but because he, according to his ability, performed the duty entrusted to him, unflinchingly, with serene courage, never disturbed, always calm, quiet and peaceful. Our friend made hosts of friends.

When I said our mortality hugged us close, I felt it in my own case. A Spiritualist ten years in advance of BROTHER COLBY, when I came to Boston it was to meet and greet him and to be associated with him and his associates in an enduring friendship ever since. I am conscious that when I walk — and I may walk here a few months longer through these streets — and pass into the editorial room of the *Banner of Light*, I shall see no more this body; my mortality hugs me close. We miss our friends because we do not see them; only the spiritual enables us to perceive them. Fortunately we are growing out of the body, depending more and more upon our spiritual intuition, upon the voices that we sometimes hear, upon the evidences of the presence of our friends which they are enabled to manifest to us; so we are growing steadily from year to year. This great truth which our BROTHER COLBY has advocated so long and to which he devoted his life, is taking root among mankind, affecting its thought, modifying the harshness of the old theology, turning people from their dependence upon theological systems, taking them away from meaningless forms of worship, and placing men where they shall be worshipers and respectors of God in their own souls.

It is a revelation to man, with God regnant in His own spirit, enforcing the idea that only goodness and virtue, those noble attributes of humanity, will stand us in good stead when we pass into the realm of the spiritual world. It is not profession merely, but it is that warm grasp of the hand which signifies the heart's friendship, and is worth more than all the prayers ever uttered.

Our friend did not discard religious forms; he respected them as helps to others, but he had no need of these crutches; he couldn't understand the necessity of forms and ceremonies; he lived the simple life of a man, was well acquainted with himself, and desired to be better acquainted with human nature. He had the geniality of a man of goodness and kindness which contributed to the happiness of others, and sympathized with their sorrows. He rarely was appealed to by any one in distress — and mediums are often in distress — whether the person belonged to the Spiritual fold or not, that his hand did not automatically seek his pocket, that he might minister to his necessities. According to his means, LUTHER COLBY was a most generous man; his heart was sympathetic, and everybody felt its goodness.

Why should I speak of a blot upon the sun? Unfortunately he was impetuous, and his impetuosity came of an excitable temper, and sometimes reason had hardly time to act before impulse to speak manifested itself, and sometimes a thoughtless word escaped; but how quick he was to apologize if he felt he had injured any one!

He was not easily imposed upon; he was a man of clear vision; he knew men when he met them, and did not allow them often to succeed in deceiving him. That was one of his marked characteristics, and in his giving he seldom gave unwisely.

But these are incidentals. We are not to analyze each other, we are to

make the best of each other under the circumstances; and how much
better it would be if, following the lead of this dear friend, we could bring
about us such genial companionship, so it would be a little taste of
heaven, and so, doing good so far as in our power lay in this world, having no fear of the future, and having discharged all our obligations, go
forward to the future opportunities of the spiritual life! What do we
know? How little; and yet our minds are reasonably active; they seem
to be limited, and we can grasp but a few subjects. Well, the time is
coming when every subject shall be within our purview, and a state of
understanding where our education may be complete. In that sphere, in
the world immortal, we shall be deathless, and go on toward perfection.
I see the folds of that banner, that *Banner of Light.* It seems to illu-
minate those who are walking in the dark valley of the shadow of death. It
has never been furled, and I hope and trust and believe that it never will
be furled. I must say this of it, that it has never been published as a
financial speculation or investment, but simply and always for the cause it
advocated. If it had been published merely as a financial venture, the
vicissitudes of the past, fires and other misfortunes, would have prevented
the flowing of that *Banner;* but whatever it might cost, it was resolved
that *The Banner* should be sustained, and I trust it will be so in the
future, and that it will be carried forward as in the past; and in memory
of our dear friend let us pledge our assistance that it shall be sustained.

ADDRESS OF MR. COBB.

Miss Dodge then sang "The Lifting of the Veil," after
which Eben Cobb, President of the America Hall Society,
Boston, addressed the people. He spoke of the true conception of physical translation which Spiritualism gives to its
adherents, and then said (among other points):

I feel that our good friend has not gone, but is translated. Our brother
died of old age, and is taken up by angel hands. How blessed is this
thought! . . .

It has been erroneously said, and is to-day, that every man — I think it
ought to have included women — is born free and equal. It is no such
thing. We all believe, I assume, that in every human being there is a
soul, and the heart of that soul, the inward spark of glory, is from the
dear God above. But there are possibilities on earth that that spark for
a time may be so covered and corroded and enchained, even at one's

birth, that the individual is far from free, but on the contrary is imprisoned, fettered, manacled, and the tender light in the soul is hidden in the glare of its environment. I allude to no particular creed, to no particular sect. I have a hard word for no one to-day, for I know that there is true religion and true goodness and whole-souled piety in every creed that the world has known; but hand-in-hand with that goodness, that charity and benevolence, what hard, cruel, rigid, adamantine chains have clanked and have been wound around the young tendrils of the budding soul to hold it tight lest it get away from some sanctified altar. . . .

There is no greatness in the world to be created by the thunder of cannon, the clashing of swords and the spread of ruin and desolation. The greatest law that we can recognize as coming from that beloved old prophet of Nazareth, the law above all others, is the law of love, which our dear friend whose mortal remains lie in this casket before us, so fully exemplified; and there is not a man or woman on earth whose life is controlled by that great guiding star, who is not entitled to be called great.

Year after year has our dear friend been. as it were, buried in his sanctum, in order to test and send out — what? Light, freedom, and a broader field of investigation for the soul; and under this benign influence has humanity been steadily advanced.

I have not for years been called upon to attend and officiate at a funeral, in connection with good ministers of the Gospel of Jesus Christ of all denominations, but what I have found that their earnest endeavor was to impress upon the hearts and souls and minds of the mourners present that their dear friends, gone, by the permission of a kind, over-ruling Providence, were allowed to return and hover about them, and sympathize with them in their joys and sorrows. . . .

From all over the civilized world, from lofty palace and humble hut, warming with tender life in fane and cathedral, came to the veteran's ears breathings of earnest orisons, freighted with heart-assurance gained by intercourse with departed loves. Glorious thought! That after long years of ceaseless toil and heroic contest toward a victory for the Higher Life, the dauntless champion could calmly survey the field and say within his soul, " Truly, the battle is won!" Fit time that his liberated spirit should join the welcoming throng beyond.

Are we sincere? Is this manifestation of memorial regard a mere service of form, or springs it from the united throb of deep, abiding love? If the latter, remember that the old General has left tried and trusty marshals still at his wonted post of duty. Let us generously aid them with a patriot's zeal, for yet will it be LUTHER COLBY's greatest joy to see the glorious old *Banner of Light* waving freely over a regenerated world.

Dr. Storer then read the resolutions forwarded for the occasion by the National Spiritualist Convention :

WASHINGTON, D. C., October 9, 1894.

The delegates of the NATIONAL SPIRITUALISTS' ASSOCIATION, in convention assembled, have heard with profound emotion of the transition of our venerable and much beloved brother, LUTHER COLBY, editor of the *Banner of Light :* Therefore,

Resolved, That in his birth to a higher condition we recognize a great spiritual truth, that while we are not permitted to mourn, we have lost from our mortal activity one of the noblest workers in our glorious Cause ; one whose life-long labors for the great truth of Spiritualism have made it possible for this Convention to assemble.

Resolved, That words are inadequate to express our appreciation of the generous heart, the ever-ready and active brain, the hand extended in charity always, and the unflinching fidelity to, and defence of, the Cause that was dearer to him than life.

Resolved, That we cannot fail to recognize the irreparable loss, in his removal from the duties that he so loved to perform ; still do we know that he has joined that noble band of spirits who aided the great work performed by him, as editor of the *Banner of Light* from its inception, and that his influence and presence will still be the abiding and controlling power of its future usefulness.

Resolved, That we tender our sympathy to his associates of the *Banner of Light* Publishing House, and to his relatives and friends, though we realize that their loss is his gain.

Be it further Resolved, That these resolutions be inscribed upon the minutes of this Convention, and a copy of same be sent to the Spiritualist papers for publication,

> W. H. BACH, St. Paul, Minn.
> M. E. CADWALLADER, Philadelphia, Pa.
> CORA L. V. RICHMOND, Chicago, Ill.
> L. P. WHEELOCK, Moline, Ill.
> DR. I. T. AKIN, Blooming Valley, Pa.

Miss Dodge then sang "Beautiful Life," after which Mr. Lyman C. Howe spoke appreciatively of him whose form was stretched before the congregation in the restful embrace of Change.

ADDRESS BY LYMAN C. HOWE.

. . . Our brother, LUTHER COLBY, has left his mark upon this world, and taken with him the love and blessings of millions who have shared in the consolations of Spiritualism, brought to their knowledge through his instrumentality.

I have known him personally over twenty years, and I gladly add my tribute to his memory; and the best thing I can say of him is that he was *a man*, with an inheritance of infinite possibilities; and in his fourscore years of life he has impressed those superior qualities of mind and heart upon many thousands for the healing of the nations.

He has come in touch with millions through his public ministrations, with thousands personally; and every one who has felt the life of his touch retains the impress of his individuality still. That impress is, and will continue to be, a modifying influence in the direction of character and its development. He was strong in convictions, and ready to carry out, according to his best understanding, the highest ideals of his life; and in his departure we shall miss all these outward, tangible expressions, and none can take his place from this time, though others, perhaps, are equally as well qualified to give direction to the work he so vigorously and successfully prosecuted; and yet others will now move in his shadow and personality, will be affected by the psychic influences of this master in their impressions, tendencies, thoughts, feelings, emotions and affections.

The best that can be said of any man is that he is loyal to his convictions, and his heart warms with love and devotion to his fellows. This can be said with emphasis of LUTHER COLBY. He was tender, sympathetic, impulsive, and generous to the helpless and needy. In Spiritualism he found an ample field for the play of his genius and the application of his high ideals and generous instincts to the improvement of the race. His soul was in his chosen work. For it he lived and labored. A happy enthusiasm inspired his efforts, and carried his convictions to the hearts of the people. He loved, thrilled, suffered, enjoyed, wept and smiled, with and for humanity. Such a presence carries the tide of emotions with it in all the works of life; and, now that he is arisen, we may expect to realize the value of these qualities continued in the same line of work whose visible agents will be his successors in the conduct of his beloved *Banner*. . . .

I gladly offer my tribute to the memory of LUTHER COLBY. He was my friend. Our relations were always pleasant, though we did not always see alike. I shall remember him as long as my individuality remains. Soon I shall follow him through that shining gate, and again we shall clasp hands and rejoice. Whether he be sitting here and listening and looking, matters not, so that we feel that his individuality survives the physical decay, and puts on a stronger armor, a higher significance, a more impressive symmetry, a more expansive expression of intelligence, a still finer and deeper manifestation of those impulses that thrilled him when his heart prompted him to deeds of love and charity unseen and unknown by the world. May we feel his presence often. May we sense and recognize his nearness to us; may we look up hopefully, trustfully, not only to him, but to others like unto him whose service has been for human emancipation, and has been fearlessly and faithfully performed; and through these may we form a closer union with that world of light which lies beyond, and become familiar with those visions of beauty and glory, and those translations of knowledge and truth that come to the soul, and thereby swing the gate somewhat wider between the two worlds. . . .

At the conclusion of the exercises the congregation gazed on the remains. Disposed around the body — which was enclosed in a casket of black cloth — were the following gentlemen, who acted as pall-bearers: Isaac B. Rich, John W. Day, Charles McArthur, Moses T. Dole, M. S. Ayer, Frederick G. Tuttle, Charles F. Fay, David W. Craig, William C. Tallman, W. S. Butler and William F. Nye. The ushers were Charles T. Wood, Marshall O. Wilcox. The funeral appointments were furnished by Mr. J. Tinkham, undertaker. Mr. H. W. Pitman — associate editor of *The Banner* — made and carried out the arrangements for the funeral. The body was taken to Forest Hills, where it was cremated. Thursday, October 11th, the ashes were interred in Mrs. Conant's lot at Forest Hills Cemetery, Boston, Mass.

CHAPTER VI.

"Thou didst fall in the field with thy silver hair,
    And a *Banner* in thy hand ;
Thou wert laid to rest from thy battles there
    By a proudly mournful band."
                            — *Mrs. Hemans's " Marshal Shewerin."*

As might naturally be expected the demise and obsequies
of Mr. Colby struck a profound and solemn chord in all
hearts devoted to the advocacy of the New Dispensation.
The brave men and women who for years had been accustomed
to see him in the van of the movement caught a quick breath
as they saw him fall, and then turned their faces like flint
once more to the front, seeking to follow his example in working out the remainder of "life's little day "; while those
younger in the movement — recognizing the value of his
labors in the past, which had prepared for them the highway
along which to tread in the discharge of incumbent duty —
involuntarily drew closer in their ranks as they moved onward.
But from both classes words of the highest esteem found utterance and publicity concerning his service on earth, and
from these kindly expressions given from time to time in the
columns of *The Banner* and elsewhere, the following are culled
as a garland to his memory.

No attempt has been made to give articles in entirety — the
extent of the field of choice precludes that ; but the extracts
here appended have been chosen as giving vent to the feelings
of the writers. To avoid repetition in the ideas expressed,
when all spoke to one purpose, and with a single aim, is well-
nigh impossible ; condensation in prose and poetic remem-

brance has been rendered obligatory. The criticism of the reader is therefore here forestalled by an appeal alike to his or her reason and affection in the premises.

In the course of an address delivered in Baltimore by W. J. COLVILLE, occurred, among other sentences, the following :

After stating that it was his special duty on that occasion to chronicle the passing from the scenes of mortal labor of LUTHER COLBY, senior editor of the *Banner of Light*, Mr. Colville proceeded :

For thirty-seven years has the *Banner of Light* been floating to the breeze, and for all that time the name of LUTHER COLBY has been prominently displayed on this fearless and progressive sheet. We well know that whenever one worker is called to his well-earned recompense in the Great Beyond, others are brought forward to fill the vacant place; but though our faith be ever so firm in the superintending guidance of infinite beneficence, we cannot feel (on the earthly side) other than sorry to miss the cheery voice and imposing presence of one whom we have learned to love by reason of the tie of sincere friendship which has for many years bound us very closely together. When your present speaker, at the early age of eighteen, commenced public work in Boston, he found LUTHER COLBY from the first a stalwart, influential friend; and through the nearly sixteen years which have intervened from November, 1878, till October, 1894, the friendship thus early formed has strengthened and perpetually increased.

But it is not of personal kindness extended to your lecturer that we desire to speak, for in a life so full of kindness as was that of our so recently ascended friend, courtesies and good-will extended to any single individual constitute but a drop in an ocean of benevolence. It was our great privilege to know MR. COLBY, not merely to enjoy a surface acquaintance with him, and therefore are we in a position to speak understandingly of the depth of his nature, and the extreme generosity and fidelity of his character.

In these days, when so many people are looking into Spiritualism and all that pertains thereto, it requires no more than a little capital to start a weekly or monthly periodical devoted to the advocacy and elucidation of Spiritual Philosophy and Phenomena; but in 1857 it needed bravery of spirit far beyond the average to face the violent and reasonless opposition which was then almost everywhere extended to advocates of Modern Spiritualism in the early years of its eventful history. From the very hour when the *Banner of Light* commenced to wave in obedience to spiritual direction, till the hour of his passing to join the innumerable company of friends and fellow-workers who have already greeted him on the "other side," MR. COLBY's heart, intellect and worldly means were all devoted to the best interests of the Cause he loved better than life.   Fair-weather advocates of any cause are numerous as mushrooms after a shower, but those who will adhere, if possible, even closer to the principles they represent when the storm of adversity presses, are rare indeed.

The *Banner of Light*, with LUTHER COLBY at its head, has been like the proverbial Jew in history — fire could not burn it, water could not drown it, though flame and flood raised their fury against it, for it had and still has a heaven-born mission to fulfil; therefore it has triumphed and will continue to triumph over the very elements of nature, and over the misguided passions of mankind.   So large and liberal, so widely and grandly comprehensive was our veteran's editorial policy, that the columns of his admirable newspaper were never defiled with insulting personalities, coarse illustrations or ribald jests. . . .

A clean, able family paper, conducted in the interests of a once highly unpopular Cause through thirty-seven years of fluctuating fortune, deserves the recognition and respect not only of Spiritualists, but of liberal thinkers everywhere; and here let us aver that multitudes of progressive thinkers the world over, though they may not have identified themselves in all cases with Spiritualism proper, have had their otherwise thorny pathway greatly smoothed through the faithful, tireless advocacy of the broadest freedom of thought and expression for which the *Banner of Light* has ever stood, and just as widely stands to-day as in the hour when the first issue was published.

True it is that MR. COLBY has had faithful and talented co-workers: but he has ever been the central magnet and efficient nucleus around which the honorable galaxy of assistants have been proud to gather. Were we to express a tenth part of what we could most sincerely and conscientiously utter at this point, we should no doubt be deemed guilty of reckless extravagance in speech, even by our most appreciative friends: but though we forbear, lest too strong eulogy should appear unwise, we urge upon the Spiritualists of the United States the erection of an abiding monument to LUTHER COLBY: not a statue in a public square in Boston, though that would be by no means inappropriate; and certainly not a useless expenditure upon a memorial urn or column in the cemetery where his ashes rest; but the liberal endowment of the paper to which he gave his best years, his time, his thought, his love, his talents, that it may be in future not only what it has been in the past, but even vastly more efficient, and truly representative. . . . The history of Spiritualism in America could not be written with the name of LUTHER COLBY left out.

HON. LUTHER R. MARSH, of Middletown, N. Y., said, in the course of a memorial tribute :

Renewed, re-invigorated, re-vitalized, freed from shackles, he enters on a new career. He looks back upon the thirty-seven years of editorial toil with satisfaction; and forward to the centuries of spiritual work before him, with joy. How small official stations are beside that he fills! . . .

In full assurance of the truth — conveyed to sight and hearing and touch and inner conviction — he did not quail before the combined attacks of the adversaries of the Cause.

He *knew* that he knew. He had reliance on himself. He had faith in his own eyes. He believed his own ears. He stood by his own judgment. Hearsay and speculation and conjecture were vain in effort to overthrow his conviction, based on knowledge. His courage was heroic. He would front the world. Secular and theologic presses might print and scatter earth-wide their fierce denunciations; they brought to his sanctum only a feeling of pity for their ignorance, and of hope for their future. Standing like a rocky pillar, conspicuous and unremoved, he has looked out upon the waters, year by year receding, and beheld the prospect brightening all around him.

In every country men have come up to his support. An abounding literature fortifies his position. New presses in America, in Europe, even in remote Australia, advocate the Cause. Sensitives start up in almost every family, and throng in every city. Camps gather their thousands in "the groves," "God's first temples." Old dogmas, man-made, are not ladled out to the crowds who seek their leaf-roofed auditoriums. Poets sing in concord. Lips "touched with celestial fire" speak forth celestial truth. In the last half of this man's life, and largely owing to his efforts, has this marvellous change been wrought. Well may he receive the benediction " Well done!" . . .

MRS. LOVE M. WILLIS, of Rochester, N. Y., wrote as follows :

It is over thirty years since I first knew MR. COLBY. I was then engaged to edit the Children's Department of the *Banner of Light*, which brought me for five years into correspondence with him. The noblest tribute I can give to him personally is that he was ever a reliable and faithful friend. Every one who has known of his public career knows that he was always true to his conviction of right and truth. He had buckled on "the armor of salvation," and he always felt like a captain leading souls forward against the hosts of error. To some of his co-workers, he seemed too aggressive, too sensitive; but he had labored so long and faithfully, and had suffered so much for truth's sake, it is no wonder that he felt keenly the misunderstandings that he had to encounter. It is one of the results of our American civilization that there is little respect for age and experience. The young feel that they know far better what the new time needs; but all must acknowledge that MR. COLBY kept abreast of the times, and gave, in the *Banner of Light,* the most candid *résumé* of the progress of the spiritual movement on the material plane that was consistent with his convictions. He devoted time and money to the cause he had espoused, and that he loved better than all temporal good. Even friendships and reputation, when weighed in the balance with duty, were found wanting.

EDITH WILLIS LINN, the talented daughter of Dr. F. L. H. and Mrs. Love M. Willis, wrote the subjoined :

TO ONE WHO HAS DEPARTED.

Cast in a grand, heroic mold,
   As old-time warriors, bold and brave,
Thou hast waged the battle for the truth,
   Men's souls from fear and gloom to save.

Not by the sword that conquest was ;
   A harder battle wageth here —
A fight against the laugh of scorn,
   And bigot's hate and cynic's sneer.

     .   .   .   .

Thy valiant soul had need of strife.
   Oh ! not for thee earth's flowers and wine.
I like to think that even now
   The conquest and the toil are thine.

Dear friend, brave soldier, fare thee well.
   Forget not earth and all her fears.
Let strength of thine renew our strength,
   And ease our hearts and dry our tears.

> From earth's ignoble, jealous life,
>   Thy soul hath risen into light.
> Thy crown awaits thee; angel hands
>   Will wrap thee in thy garments bright.
>
> Peace shall be thine that comes from power;
>   And victory thine that follows strife.
> Our hearts are better for thy love,
>   The world is nobler for thy life!

DR. FRED. L. H. WILLIS, after speaking of his abiding memories of MR. COLBY, and the hour of his (Willis's) persecution and expulsion from Harvard College because of his mediumship, says:

He found me broken in body, and crushed in spirit, just rallying from a fearful attack of brain-fever, the result of the intense excitement I had been laboring under, and the unjust verdict of the Faculty. I felt that my life was hopelessly wrecked.

MR. COLBY was then in the prime of his life, full of mental and physical vigor, full of enthusiasm for the new faith whose facts and philosophy had been overwhelmingly demonstrated to him through the marvelous mediumship of Mrs. Fanny Conant and others.

He had just heard the decision of the Faculty, and burning with indignation came out to see the victim of it.

It was a memorable interview. His brave words encouraged and uplifted me. He convinced me that all was not lost, as I had imagined; that thousands of friends were rallying about me, and that the angel world was behind me to care for and protect me; and then, with the remarkable prophetic power he gave proofs of possessing, even at that early day, he mapped out my future career, and most accurately predicted the part I was to play in the New Dispensation being then in process of inauguration.

From that day he was my faithful, true friend. He revealed to me a side of his nature that he allowed but few to obtain glimpses of. There was a child-like, tender, loving side to his nature that his external manner seldom revealed.

To me he typified and illustrated the best phases of human nature in many respects. He was sympathetic with all sufferings, generous in his impulses, cosmopolitan in spirit, claiming no right or privilege for himself that he did not wish to share with every child of humanity. . . .

The services he rendered to Spiritualism cannot be estimated. He threw heart and soul into his work. The *Banner of Light* was to him what an idolized child is to a fond parent. His devotion to it was supreme. . . .

PROF. J. JAY WATSON, of New York, in a letter relating MR. COLBY's generosity toward the Indians *et al,* —after speaking in terms of the highest appreciation of his character as a man and a worker, said :

As he drew near the end of his earthly pilgrimage, his warm heart seemed to grow still more tender toward everyone, and his extreme sensitiveness to increase in like ratio.

At our last interview I was alluding to some accident that had occurred. Suddenly wheeling around and looking me intently in the eye, he calmly, and in a most subdued voice, asked, "*Are* there any accidents?" To this pertinent question I could only reiterate Col. Robert G. Ingersoll's famous saying, "Let's be honest and say we don't know." Well may Gerald Massey's touching lines so aptly applied by Mr. Thomas Lees in his recent letter to *The Banner,* again be quoted :

> "Of such as he was, there be few on earth,
> Of such as he was, there be many in Heaven;
> And life is all the sweeter that he lived,
> And death is all the fairer that he died,
> And Heaven is all the brighter that he's there."

JAMES M. PEEBLES, of San Diego, Cal., a life-long friend of MR. COLBY — to whose views concerning his mediumship reference has before been made, said on one other occasion :

LUTHER COLBY, after careful and critical investigation, became a Spiritualist — when it cost something to be a pronounced Spiritualist. And yet, from the hour of his conviction and conversion to the grand truth, he never for a moment swerved, nor faltered in defending it with voice and pen. No matter how dark the cloud, he saw the sun shining above it. No indifference chilled his zeal; no vague reports prejudiced his judgment; no disaster checked his soul-felt ardor, nor cooled his intense love for the grand uplifting truths engermed in and connected with the Spiritual Philosophy. He will live in the history of Spiritualism on earth immortal, for no truth can die nor principle perish.

Mortal he was, and momentarily impulsive he may have been, when weighed down by the burdens of pressing responsibilities and by a daily flood of letters, bringing, many of them, scheming, selfish auras; and yet, under all these trying conditions and struggles for the right and the true, there beat a heart as gentle and tender as a woman's.

LUTHER COLBY, though a man of strong convictions, ever counselled peace, and the exercise of that charity toward others that "endureth all things."

Though for four years editor of the Western Department of the *Banner of Light*, and corresponding for its columns for thirty years, more or less — intimately acquainted necessarily with the proprietors and editors of *The Banner*, I can conscientiously say I have never known more honorable, upright men ; and, of LUTHER COLBY, I unhesitatingly say that for good intentions, for sterling integrity, for tenacious memory, for willingness to praise rather than censure others, for charity toward those who differed from him, for sympathy toward sensitive, persecuted mediums and for consecration to the truth of Spiritualism, he had no superior. . . .

JENNIE LEYS wrote for *The Banner* this, as her tribute to

LUTHER COLBY.

The angels' Banner-Bearer, crowned with light !
　　Fronting with fearless faith the frowning world,
　　He held aloft God's ensign, wide unfurled,
To shed Heaven's peace on Death's despairing night.

Through Truth's long war that standard never fell
　　From its ideal, so sublimely true ;
　　But brought immortal life and love in view
By the great message it was charged to tell.

No dark word marred his *Banner's* sacred scroll.
　　Each medium's steadfast friend, through storm or shine
　　He mantled all with love and trust divine —
The golden aura of his own grand soul.

Ah ! who can count the hearts he comforted ?
　　Earth's stricken lives he raised, and stayed their tears,
　　To sing the new song from the spirit-spheres :
" Our loved ones live ! they live ! there are no dead ! "

All life grew bright at that celestial song !　.
　　Thou heart of gold, whom trial tarnished not,
　　View now the heavenly work those full years wrought :
The whole world welcomes now the spirit-throng.

Behold! thy people rise and call thee blest!
   Their love and praise eternal round thee beam.
   Thrice-sacred now the Cause we hold supreme,
Since thou, too, hast become a spirit-guest.

Hearken the earth's acclaim to thy new height:
   Well done, oh noble soul, thy glorious part!
   Beyond the shining veil! yet still thou art
The angels' Banner-Bearer, crowned with light!

GILES B. STEBBINS, of Detroit, Mich., one of the sturdy toilers for reform in its various branches, wrote as follows in summing up his conception of the subject of this volume:

Few men have been faithful and abundant in labor for a high end for so long a time. For thirty-seven years he was the guiding genius of his beloved *Banner of Light* — to set before a waiting world, in its columns, the power and presence and influence of the dwellers in the spirit-world, the central and inspiring idea and aim of his increasing efforts. He sought to save humanity by giving light from the spirit-world for their help and guidance. He was faithful to the supernal intelligences, in the full belief that thus he could best be sure of their help in his daily life, and he made the *Banner of Light* known and recognized as valuable by spiritual thinkers in every country of the civilized world.

He wrought in his own way and by his own light, as all must, and those who could not always agree with him recognized and honored his large usefulness.

GEORGE A. FULLER, of Worcester, Mass., President of the State Association of Spiritualists, said:

How joyous must have been his meeting with the great souls with whom he had been associated in the years gone by in all his laudable efforts to uplift and bless humanity. In the truest sense of the term he was the friend of all humanity, and in an especial sense the friend of all mediums. Many here will miss his kindly words of appreciation, and his substantial assistance to those who have given their lives and all for Spiritualism. May his spirit inspire those in whose hands *The Banner* will now be entrusted. May the same kindly spirit pervade its columns, and may it still continue as the light-bearer of the advance guards of our Spiritual Philosophy.

A. B. FRENCH, of Clyde, O., an eloquent and widely-known advocate of the Spiritual Cause, thus spoke of him "who has gone unto his place":

LUTHER COLBY leaves to us the rich legacy of a heroic life. He has touched this world, and it has and will feel the thrill of his spirit. He has builded for himself a monument more enduring than bronze or granite. Artless as a child; sympathetic as a loving woman; generous as the noonday sun, and faithful to his convictions as are the changeless stars to a changing earth, his work will live after him!

Emerson, the Plato of the Occident, has said: "The way to speak and write what shall not go out of fashion is to speak and write sincerely."

MR. COLBY brought to his work the sincerity of his great heart. To him Spiritualism was light and air, singing bird and summer shower. For it he toiled in unselfish devotion. He was truly the medium's friend, and many will miss the aid of his generous hand.

As the setting sun lies down upon a sea crimsoned with its own beauty, so LUTHER COLBY has enshrined himself in the hearts of his thousands of friends, and taken another step toward the unread secret of the universe.

Let us not mourn the fate of Spiritualism because he has gone up higher. The Elijah of every great cause drops from his ascending chariot his unsoiled mantle for others to wear.

So the work goes forward when the workman dies. In the wake of every wave which breaks upon the shore, there follows another in quick succession, equally as strong. *The Banner* will not droop by his transition. Another star has been added to its luminous folds, to shine with White, Brittan, Pierpont, and others of the old guard. *Let us who still journey through sun and shade to our release, rally to its standard and help to keep it firm.*

JOSEPH D. STILES, the remarkably successful platform test medium, wrote from Weymouth, Mass., this bit of history, with its accompanying prophecy so grandly fulfilled:

From the martyrdom of bitter experience and trial has LUTHER COLBY passed to the sure reward awaiting his faithful service here. The world may never rear monument nor pillar above his ashes, but the monument he has reared in countless grateful hearts will live ages after granite or marble has crumbled to dust.

I had the privilege of being in the Old Melodeon when the first copies of *The Banner* were distributed, and as I hastily perused the contents I turned to a lady friend by my side, with whom BROTHER COLBY became well acquainted in after years, with the remark: "That paper will be a wondrous power in the world!" Subsequent years have verified the prophecy.

From a tribute furnished *The Banner* by GEORGE A. BACON, of Washington, D. C., an intimate friend of MR. COLBY from the foundation of that paper, these paragraphs are excerpted:

The numberless, outspoken tributes to his memory, from hearts rich with human sympathy — from the humblest as from the highest names known to our ranks, even from some who for years had not regarded him as a friend, but whose recent words of commendation are alike creditable to their heads and hearts — these impromptu tributes are the best evidences as to the character and value of BROTHER COLBY'S life-work in the Cause that dominated his every thought.

But however hearty the bestowal of praise, nothing has been said that was not fully merited. Whatever he felt was his duty, or what he regarded was right, he did it fearlessly, though consequences might not always be pleasant either to him or to his friends. . . .

Of sturdy build and physical inheritance, his thought was practical, his outlook broad, his mind of universal cast. Strong in his friendships, he hated every semblance of ingratitude; stern of judgment, he was tender as a woman.

He loved justice, and abhorred all forms of oppression. While his active sympathies reached out to every class, he felt to specially condemn the nation's treatment of our Indian wards. Hand in hand with his intelligent efforts to impart spiritual light and knowledge, are to be remembered his numberless acts of gracious kindness and generosity toward others in material things. With only very limited means, he was constantly doing good in this direction, far more than many with independent resources: Unremittingly contributing to the necessities of some worthy person or cause till after his own affairs were seriously crippled — these unselfish acts stand out like stars at night and reflect his goodness of heart. They bear record of him on earth and in heaven.

May his minor defects of character but serve to improve our own, and his many greater virtues be cherished and emulated by all who knew him; thus will the world continue to be better for his having lived in it.

THOMAS LEES, of Cleveland, O., who as a prominent Spiritualist worker in the West, and voluminous correspondent for

The Banner, had long been known to MR. COLBY, wrote concerning his transition:

Early in the week the unexpected intelligence reached Cleveland, through friend Wm. F. Nye of New Bedford, that the veteran Spiritualist and senior editor of the *Banner of Light*, LUTHER COLBY, had left his many friends on this mundane sphere to join the multitudinous ones who had preceded him to spirit-life.

Certainly no man was better prepared for the journey, for in the last half of the eighty years of his earth-life he had had a most wonderful experience, proving on all occasions faithful to the sacred trust reposed in him by the spirit-world. His was indeed a record to be proud of. Nobly and courageously he has stood during that long period by that *Banner of Light* (the symbol of all that is grand and good in Modern Spiritualism) that he and Brother Berry flung to the breeze in Boston in 1857.

MOSES HULL, then doing most effective service for the Cause in Cleveland, also wrote:

Although LUTHER COLBY was, as the Bible says, "old and full of years," and I may add, fully ripe for the spirit side of life, yet when I think of his having gone to the "great majority" I feel a wave of sadness come over me. He was the first editor in our Cause, when I came tremblingly into it, to take me by the hand and give me a word of cheer. He was ever true to the Cause we loved and to its workers.

He will be missed particularly by the old veterans, who are being so rapidly thinned out among the workers here. The few who are left of us are getting lonesome; yet amid our loneliness we rejoice to know that we are hourly drawing nearer to that host on the other side who loved, labored and suffered for the Cause here.

I wonder if these old, faithful toilers, among whom BROTHER COLBY is in the front ranks, will not, inasmuch as they know so much about the work *here*, organize a special work in connection with that of those who remain to fight the spiritual battles on this side of the river.

ALBERT MORTON, himself an old Bostonian, who has for years resided in San Francisco, but who is now a resident of Summerland, Cal., wrote from thence the following in a tribute to MR. COLBY's work, and the value of *The Banner's* message department:

He was the first to open a public way through which the decarnated spirits could transmit messages of comfort to their bereaved friends, and in doing that he was instrumental in doing a grand, Christ-like work, bringing rest to the weary, comfort to the afflicted, and hope to the despairing. All this has been done through the Message Department of the *Banner of Light.* The Pharisee and Levite have passed this work with sneers and contempt, but the good Samaritan continued to bind up the wounds and apply the healing balsam regardless of the criticism of captious or cynical critics. It is an evidence of the generosity of the managers that in this department of *The Banner* they have annually expended, ever since it was founded, means sufficient to more than cover the entire cost of the publication of other papers ; and this work has been performed by Luther Colby and his associates, with but little return to them, aside from the grand reward arising from the consciousness of a good work being faithfully performed.

The genuineness of the messages was at first thoroughly tested by the editor, and they were not published until their correctness could be established, which course was continued until their reliability became too well confirmed to require the delay and expense attendant on such investigation.

The objections frequently raised to the common and illiterate messages sometimes given indicate a want of feeling and small spirituality on the part of the critic. An ancient medium did not deem the time wasted which he spent in comforting a poor woman at a well in Galilee, and, in the esteem of grand, philanthropic spirits, perhaps the message conveying comfort to a despairing mother or wife, even if clothed in uncouth language, may be considered as a greater service to humanity than many self-glorifying strainings for scientific reputation. . . .

This one department of *The Banner*, founded by Luther Colby, is more worthy of being commemorated by an enduring monument than the acts of those whose lives have been glorified in proportion to their ability to direct armies and slaughter men.

Our friend was hampered in all his grand life-work, but he has passed beyond the fetters of materiality, "entered into rest." the rest only to be found by one with his aspirations and honest earnestness of purpose in labors for the elevation of others, unfettered by conditions.

Emma Hardinge Britten and her husband, William Britten, of England, put themselves on record as subjoined :

To every Spiritualist throughout the world the *Banner of Light* has in some measure brought comfort, warning, instruction and good cheer —

but it is only to such long-tried, personal friends as the writers of this article that the human and personal worth of LUTHER COLBY as a judicious friend. adviser — we might almost say "a Father in Israel" — was truly known. . . .   During all trials, good, honest, brave-hearted LUTHER COLBY steered the mighty ship of Spiritualism bravely and faithfully through all the shoals and reefs of internal, as well as external, storm and tempest into triumph and glory. We, the writers, both unite in the fervent wish that we had a hundred more LUTHER COLBYS in our ranks; while we send after him our fervent blessings and the confident assurance that in a few brief and transitory years of time we shall all meet again in

The spacious grand plantation,

where there will be

No more desperate endeavors,
No more separating evers,
No more desolating nevers,
Over there.

Not very long after these kindly remembrances and heart-blessings were expressed, the noble woman, Emma Hardinge Britten, who has from the earliest days of the movement been a Colossus of spiritual power for the Cause, was called upon to say the inevitable earthly "farewell" to Dr. Britten, who "passed beyond the veil," to "the spacious grand plantation" in the Better Land. May God and angels guide the steps of his sorrowing widow, till she again shall meet her loved one "over there!"

WM. BRUNTON, of Malden, Mass., wrote the annexed in respectful memory:

LUTHER COLBY.

Good soul and blest, whose one delight and praise
    Was work for those who in high regions dwell;
    Whose messages thy *Banner* brave would tell,
And fill with golden light the passing days;
Upon thy work for years on years we gaze,
    So proud to see it grow and all excel;
    Brave veteran, thy work indeed is well,
And of itself a monument will make!

Go to thy home on high; all there are friends;
　Glad welcome waits thy footsteps in that land;
Each worker here to thee his greeting sends.
　And by thy purposed aim would faithful stand:
How blest was earth because of thy true love,
More blessed yet for it the life above!

The angel-world is not so far from ours:
　Through thee we learnt its friendliness divine;
　Its dawning light upon our world did shine.
Its kindly hands bestrewed our way with flowers:
Thy soul pursued its path to Eden bowers.
　It heard sweet voices speak in tones benign.
　It knew what influences true entwine
Our lives, what force of love their love empowers!
For all thy help to struggling truth and worth,
　For all thy sympathy in hours of need,
For all the good thy labors brought to birth.
　We bless and praise thy honored name indeed;
And evermore the Cause the past will scan
To prize thee, worker wise — true, noble man!

J. FRANK BAXTER, the widely-known platform test medium, singer and orator, on hearing of the decease of MR. COLBY wrote the appended, which was truly "A Medium's Tribute," and spoke the feelings of many of the army of public workers not here named:

Taking up a paper, my eyes at once fell upon the announcement that our loved friend and arduous and devoted co-worker had left us. I was saddened, and somewhat surprised; and yet, really, from his known condition and his ripe age, I was rather prepared. I had frequently of late thought and said: "Mr. Colby, I am afraid, is near the end of his useful career." Gone — yes! As the nuts from full maturity drop from the trees, so he, rich in worthy wisdom and full of years, has ripened to the completion of earth-need, and his interior being has passed on to the spiritual, leaving the useless case behind. We will tenderly lay the latter away; but rich are our memories not only, but our treasures. for his having lived and we having known him. While we are more or less saddened to think his material presence is no more with us — so associated have we been with it — yet our knowledge makes us look philosophically upon this

change called death, and to see in it an event in a continuous life of his
spirit; and leads us in thought and vision to follow that spirit to possible
careers in the eternal realm. What a greeting must have been his!
What a rejoicing, after all!

At the Annual Convention of the Massachusetts State
Association of Spiritualists held in Boston, at the First Spiritual Temple (corner Newbury and Exeter Streets), January 1,
1895, the Committee on Resolutions on the transition of
LUTHER COLBY made the subjoined report (unanimously
adopted) at the afternoon session (published in *The Banner*
for January 5th):

Whereas: In the fulness of time and in accordance with natural law it
has been the privilege of LUTHER COLBY — the standard-bearer of Spiritualism in America, the loyal and faithful friend of mediums, and the
stanch advocate of the principles and truths of immortality as enunciated
by communicating spirits from the Higher Life — to pass to the activities
and enjoyments of the Spiritual World; and realizing that in his removal
the Cause of Spiritualism loses from the mundane sphere an indomitable
worker, an earnest defender of Truth, and a financial supporter of
mediums and laborers generally in the field of Spiritualism, according to
his means; therefore, be it

Resolved: That the Massachusetts State Association, in convention
assembled, this first day of January, 1895, places on record in its archives,
and before the world, through the columns of the spiritual press, its deep
and sincere regret at the material and intellectual loss it and the public
have sustained in the transition of such a noble, unselfish and able advocate of the Cause we love as LUTHER COLBY, the veteran editor of the
Banner of Light.

Resolved: That while we recognize that our loss is his gain, yet we feel
that although others will carry on the work that he has laid down, and do
so according to their own light, and in a manner creditable to Spiritualism
and honorable to themselves, yet there can never be but *one* LUTHER COLBY
and that it will be many years before the Cause will rally from the effects of
the loss sustained in the ascension of the venerable man we honor and love.

Resolved: That these resolutions be placed on the records of the Massachusetts State Association, and that a copy be furnished the *Banner
of Light* and other spiritual journals for publication.

MRS. R. S. LILLIE,
WOODBURY C. SMITH, *Committee.*
MRS. M. T. LONGLEY,

The veteran Spiritualist, WILLIAM FOSTER, JR., of Providence, R. I., in speaking of the personal loss he felt in the transition of his old comrade, said:

Our friendship covered a period of some twenty-five years; and it was a friendship of the soul. Many have been our conferences at the National and Crawford Houses, extending far into the night; also at the editorial rooms. At our first meeting he received me with warm cordiality, and as our acquaintance continued, I was stirred by the unselfishness of his nature, and his devotion to truth as he saw it. It was refreshing to commune with him; there seemed to come a baptism of the spirit — an uplifting into an atmosphere of a transcendental quality — the realm of the ethereal, which made life more radiant, and illumined the tomb with more than rainbow glories, because thereby the spirit passes into immortal life.

I loved LUTHER COLBY, as I ever did those large-hearted men who stood on the watch-towers, holding beacon-lights for the race.

G. W. KATES wrote:

As the friend of mediums everywhere, he (MR. COLBY) will not lose any opportunity in spirit to extend sympathy and help. As a brother editor, the spiritual fraternity found him helpful; especially so do we now pay tribute to his many kind and generous acts in aid of our work in editing *Light for Thinkers* some years ago in the South.

WALTER HOWELL wrote, on hearing of the decease:

Many hearts have been bereft of a sympathizing friend; but our loss is his infinite gain, and while we mourn his departure from the world of sense, the world of souls rejoices in his new-born happiness! . . . The sunlight of LUTHER COLBY's spirit will continue to illumine the pages of that *Banner of Light* he labored so zealously to unfurl in this valley of shadows. May his mantle fall upon shoulders who shall wear it with honor to the cause he loved so well, and with reverence for him who has laid it aside forever.

J. W. FLETCHER expressed himself in the subjoined, and other sentences, when speaking of MR. COLBY's demise. After referring to the past history of the Cause, he said:

The spirit-world was brought into relationship with the earth-world, and demanded that means could be employed by which the glad tidings of continued life could be given to humanity. At such a moment the *Banner of Light* was unfolded to the breeze, and from that day until now it has been the advocate of pure, unadulterated Spiritualism, and heaven grant it may long continue as such. LUTHER COLBY, WM. BERRY, WM. WHITE and MRS. CONANT are all names identified with its success; and the astute management of ISAAC B. RICH, so many years associated with MR. COLBY, has done much to make that great journal what it is.

A religion that is good to *die* by is worth having. So Spiritualism proved to MR. COLBY.

J. J. MORSE, the celebrated orator in trance, or normal condition, who during his first visit from England formed a life-long friendship for MR. COLBY, bore this testimony:

Not many have enjoyed the privilege, as has the writer, of a personal and somewhat intimate acquaintance with the faithful and warm-hearted man who has lately ascended to the higher state. For nineteen years, less three months, there was a sustained friendship between us, since, to me, our memorable meeting in his Boston office, in January, 1875. Never has my opinion of the frank, honest, true-hearted man I found him, wavered.

The wise counsel, the friendly guidance and practical friendship, bestowed then and many times after, fix LUTHER COLBY in my mind — as it must, and does, in all who knew him best — as a man whom it was a privilege to know; as a friend whose friendship it was an honor to possess.

While the matter has not been specially noted in the preceding pages, LUTHER COLBY was a scion of one of the oldest families in New England, of whom a correspondent to the *Amesbury News* said some years since:

Anthony Colby was the ancestor of all the various families of that name in this vicinity. The house and homestead of [the now deceased] Obadiah Colby, situated on Ferry Street, Amesbury, is the identical house and premises which Anthony Colby bought in 1654 of Thomas Macy, and has been held and occupied by his descendants down to the present time.

HUDSON TUTTLE, in a memorial article, presented the following sentences instinct with appreciative thought and spiritual significance:

He became an advocate of the new philosophy of life here and hereafter when to do so required more than ordinary courage, and succeeded in making the journal in which he promulgated its principles respected in all civilized lands. It was ever held to the high ideal, representing the true spirit of Spiritualism — its divine, all-embracing charity, its justice and freedom from falliable judgment and personalities, its advocacy of principles above party or individual interests, its generous assistance of the weak and fearlessness of the powerful.

Well do I remember a day we passed together at Chelsea Beach. *The Banner* had gone to press, and like a boy escaped from a hard task he unbent for a day of rest he considered he had well earned. Full of pleasantry, with quaint puns and observations, the day was only too short, and we tarried until the full moon arose out of the restless waves that sparkled in silver and flashed on the beach with the incoming tide. Then on the veranda of the hotel, looking out over the mystic ocean, so like that which laves the shores of earthly life, he gave me the story of the origin and growth of his journal, his burdens and trials, and with the most unbounded faith referred to the grand spirits who had it in charge. He was weak, and the at times opposing forces nearly crushed him, yet with the spirit-world holding up his arm he felt himself invincible. And who will deny this? If the conduct of our lives is in accord with the highest spiritual teachings, and fitted to be companions of angels, we are led by them, no power on earth can turn us aside. . . .

As I would rejoice at the coming of a ship into port from the tempestuous sea, I rejoice that after many years of devoted labor he has passed on to a higher plane, where the dreams of this life may become grand realities.

Mrs. A. B. Severance, for years renowned as a psychometrist at White Water, Wis., and who had long enjoyed a personal friendship with the deceased, wrote :

Spiritualists throughout the world will unite in their sympathies, expressed or unexpressed to the *Banner of Light* workers since the passing away of Brother Luther Colby. In the realm of spiritual thought his was a wonderful mind. *As a friend to mediums there never lived a more true and faithful one.* How honest, earnest and effectual his service has been ! His love and work for humankind will still continue.

As our great spiritual toilers pass on to swell the ranks of grand and noble minds in spirit-life, others come in to fill their places, and the work will continue until all shall truly know that there is no death.

Mrs. M. S. Townsend Wood wrote a poetic tribute to his memory, from which the subjoined stanzas are extracted:

   .   .   .   .

> Mustered out of earth service to labors above;
> And crowned with the blessings of Infinite Love;
> How thousands will meet thee, and welcome thee there,
> Who have read in *The Banner* their answer to prayer;
> Who have passed from the mortal and found it all true —
> *That each one receives what in justice is due.*

> The *Banner of Light*, oh! long may it wave;
> Sustained by true natures as earnest and brave
> As he who has gone from the scenes of earth-strife
> To join the grand army in spiritual life.
> May charity breathe through its pages to all,
> While love weaves the mantle that ever must fall
> O'er weak ones who struggle through sorrow and sin,
> Through the tempest of life with discords and din.

> Mustered out; but we know he will work with us still,
> And help us each duty of life to fulfil,
> And will wave a new *Banner* from mansions above,
> With its motto of Peace, and its teachings of Love;
> With its columns of messages, coming to bless,
> From our loved who have gone to that sweet land of rest.
> We mourn not to-day for this soldier so brave;
> No spirit like his can be held by the grave,
> But onward and upward, forever and aye,
> He will march in the light of eternity's day!

Mr. and Mrs. Milton Rathbun spoke concerning the passage of Mr. Colby to Higher Life:

We could but rejoice that he had entered into his reward for so many years of faithful, efficient service in the cause of Spiritualism; but with our joy for his promotion came sorrow for the loss of a loyal friend, a grand, untiring worker to advance the truth in all of its varied phases; a defender of true mediums; a stanch supporter and helper of the oppressed and downtrodden; a kind, tender-hearted, sincere gentleman in all the walks of life. We had hoped that he might be spared to us years to come ; but for him we feel it is better as decreed, for his inheritance must be bright and abundant, because well earned by the unremitting and indefatigable labor and self-sacrifice of so many long years.

May his mantle fall upon those who will cheerfully carry forward his life-work. May the brave old *Banner* increase in its power for good, in circulation, and reach eventually the remotest corners of the earth. We are sure that its influence will be fostered by our friend, who gladly responded to the call, " Come up higher." May we all emulate his example in loyalty, fealty, industry, charity and good deeds.

FRED. L. HILDRETH, a noted worker in the Children's Progressive Lyceum field, wrote a memorial to " Our Teacher, LUTHER COLBY," from which the appended is excerpted.

And so the soul that through the long, long years
    Stood first in Freedom's ranks — untrammelled, free !
Hath crossed the rainbow bridge to brighter lands :
    While, as our eyes peer 'cross the mystic sea,
His feet tread onward up Progression's path,
    Toward the far summit, crowned with sweetest flowers
Culled by his hands amid earth's weary hearts,
    And nurtured by his friends in angel bowers.

.   .   .   .

So we must say good-night, but not good-by,
    To one who bore life's load with willing heart.
The ties your noble deeds wove round our souls
    Are only changed — we cannot let them part !
Grand, fearless soul ! Life's mission well fulfilled —
    A ripened harvest in the long-drawn years :
It would not dim the sunshine if my muse
    Brought flowers to your grave in place of tears.

Good-night ! my friend — the bells in angel lands
    Ring a glad peal, a welcome kind to you ;
And your garb, worn while toiling here with us,
    Will change from earthly dark to brighter hue !
In many a land your dear old *Banner* waves,
    Bearing its buds of promise, sweet and bright :
Your buds have bloomed, and many a swelling heart
    Bids you God speed ! and kindliest good-night !

Dr. E. A. SMITH, President of the Queen City Park Camp Association, and the Vermont State Spiritualist Association, wrote :

From friends far and near the words of sympathy and love seem to come; and it is rare indeed that such a universal testimony is given to the worth and courage of one man, as well as the appreciation of his great work, and is in itself a proof of the hold he had on the affections and esteem of Spiritualists the world over.

I have known MR. COLBY for many years, and I ever found him kind and courteous, always most willing to help any young society and give it a place and a name in his paper, and never refusing to publish anything that might assist the efforts of others in the great Cause he loved so well. I know that I voice the sentiments of every member of our State Association, when I say that we mourn his loss as that of a dear friend and brother. And now honored and revered by all he has gone to that higher life and larger sphere of labor, full of years and honors; yet we know he is with us still.

His name is a household word wherever the *Banner of Light* is known and read, and though loving friends may erect marble tablets to his memory, I think there can be no monument so fitting or so enduring as the pages of *The Banner* he so long and so nobly carried.

MATILDA CUSHING SMITH contributed to *The Banner,* as her token to his memory, the following acrostic, dealing with the paper, the establishing and conducting of which had been MR. COLBY's life work :

Bearer of comforting words of cheer,
And joyous tidings from friends beyond;
Nearer to earth thou bringest heaven;
Newly cemented love's severed bond.
Ever new thoughts thou art sending forth,
Rays to illumine the misty earth;

Out of the old, with constant care,
Faithfully building temples rare;

Lifting men's burdens, and bringing light
Into the homes once darker than night;
Giving out knowledge of untold worth;
Heaven's own messenger, fearing naught;
Truth's standard-bearer enlightening earth.

S. H. NELKE wrote, regarding the labors of MR. COLBY and his co-worker, Mr. Rich, in the following appreciative manner:

Any one who has followed the ups and downs of the *Banner of Light* must have become acquainted with the struggles of MR. LUTHER COLBY and his partner, Mr. Isaac B. Rich; and those who were permitted to look behind the curtain know that the losses of the concern from time to time would in their extended history figure up to such an amount as would be surprising.

If the readers of *The Banner* take this into consideration, it will surely stimulate them to thank LUTHER COLBY, the man who had not alone the conviction but the courage to give to the world the truths of the ever-lasting life and love, in spite of all the opposition and losses he had to encounter.

And so, readers, you, who are, indeed, mostly benefited by the publication of the noble *Banner of Light*, stand by this journal; show your appreciation of the grand work of the noble founder, LUTHER COLBY! Let no harm befall this great monument of truth and love; stand shoulder to shoulder in support of it!

ANNIE LORD CHAMBERLAIN, the veteran physical medium, wrote:

I feel his loss very keenly. He has ever been a true, kind friend to me. I first met him when I was only fifteen years old, and stopping at Daniel Farrar's.. He came there with Mr. William Berry, and I think Mr. William White also, to attend some of my seances. He was much pleased then, and has since always been an advocate of my mediumship. It seemed to please him, and I am glad it did.

In the early days of his sickness he wrote me a kind letter from the Crawford House, which I shall always highly prize.

He has done a good work, has been true and faithful, and now his spirit has gone where it will receive a just recompense.

LUTHER COLBY will never be forgotten.

ALONZO DANFORTH wrote:

Many are the encomiums called forth by the transition to spirit-life of our standard-bearer and co-worker, LUTHER COLBY. Who has done more than he to prove the undeniable certainty of a continuous life, through the columns of the *Banner of Light?* Humanity is better for the part he has taken in the life of this century. We remember his integrity, his earnestness, his kindliness of heart, his fidelity to his friends. He had the courage to obey his conscience. He was possessed of the determination to do right because it was right. In moving in a straight, even though frequently an unpopular channel, it is easy to float with the current, but to breast it requires both strength and boldness, and these traits he possessed.

May the life of LUTHER COLBY be an example for our children; may his name be kept in grateful remembrance by all who knew the work he accomplished, and when we read the shining list of the honored names of those who fought the good fight bravely and well, LUTHER COLBY'S name shall not be missed.

H. A. BUDINGTON wrote:

A long career of eminent worth on earth has ended. There are heroes and heroes. To espouse an extremely unpopular truth, because new, in the face of society's sneer, and to stand true to it, through long years of hate, contempt and social ostracism, stamps any man or woman a hero of the loftiest kind.

The revelations of spirit-communion are so strong a corrective of the prevailing religions of this planet, that the mind educated in the traditions of the past could not at first accept them. Only the few of the most receptive attitude early perceived their naturalness. BROTHER COLBY, with admirable courage and noble self-sacrifice of worldly praise, was one of the first to accept and to proclaim openly the New Philosophy.

What struggles he had with obtuse or obstinate bigots. What a gigantic task to keep the *Banner of Light* at the masthead, in such a sea of opposition! But he won! And how glorious will be his life in the higher world. He has now gone where his devotion and his labors will be appreciated.

THE VETERAN SPIRITUALISTS' UNION at a meeting held October 10th at Gould Hall, Boston, adopted the following *in memoriam*, the same being presented by President Storer:

The Veteran Spiritualists' Union, by unanimous vote, hereby enter upon their records this memorial tribute to the life, character and usefulness of our brother, LUTHER COLBY, the veteran editor of the *Banner of Light*, and a life member of this Association.

For nearly forty years his editorship of that journal, devoted to the advocacy and illustration of Spiritualism, has made it an authority upon all phases of the phenomena, and the scope of its philosophy. Not only the valuable articles from his own pen, but those which his able advocacy of the subject attracted from the most intelligent sources, have created a public opinion in its favor throughout America, and in distant lands.

Our brother was distinguished for the simplicity of his life, his genial manners, and the sympathetic interest which he felt for the poor and destitute. Above all other interests, he held that the promulgation of the knowledge of man's inherent immortality, the intimate relations of mortals and spirits, based upon the identity of human needs, and the interdependence of each upon all, in a natural order of evolution, was the most important knowledge that the mind can grasp. To this work his life was devoted.

We recognize our loss of his visible presence, but rejoice in his translation to a higher sphere of existence where those who are allied in thought and purpose form the happy spheres of the spiritual life.

Ed. S. Varney wrote :

Allow me to express my deepest sympathy for the loss sustained by the paper, as well as by the entire spiritualistic world. in the passing away of our tried and true standard-bearer, Luther Colby.

Yet, thanks be to the angel world, you and I, as Spiritualists, know that "to die is gain," and that Mr. Colby after a long life of good deeds in the body, has passed on to the land of joy and reunion, fully ripened for the beautiful, heavenly harvesting that awaits him.

For my part, no words can fitly express what he has been to me; in soul development: in sorrow, assuagement! But his priceless *Banner*, which I shall always take, will keep his dear memory forever fresh.

Sarah A. Byrnes wrote :

What a glad welcome his spirit must have had as he entered his spirit-home! What he felt as a knowledge of spirit-life must have had a glorious revelation for him. We know he has earned a generous reward, and we will make *our* faith as steadfast as he desired *his* should be — truly ripened for the harvest of the new life.

Jennie B. Hagan-Jackson said :

I do not write an expression of regret that the kind-hearted man, Luther Colby, has gone home; for I know the deeds of love and charity he performed have all been placed to his credit in the land whither he has gone.

PROF. ALEXANDER WILDER, on learning of MR. COLBY's demise, wrote to *The Banner* a memorial in which occurred the following outspoken and highly appreciative sentences :

It took me by surprise; I had never reflected that such a thing could occur. He had seemed to me a perennial character, to whom there might be autumn and winter, but certainly would always be a spring-time. So far as I knew him, he was awake to criticise whatever he felt to be wrong and oppressive; and on the alert to point out danger, but never vindictive, unkind or unforgiving.

As an editor I admired him for his sagacity, tact and excellent sense. While making a journal adapted to the tastes and minds of the readers, he was always aiming at the same time to exalt them to higher views and conceptions of the true and the right.

The Banner, in his hands, was the vigorous adversary of abuses and wrongs in the department of government and general affairs. Oppressive legislation [medical and otherwise] was pointed out, both as to its imminence and resultant mischiefs. . . .

I honor him, too, for his repeated utterances against the vaccination enormity. I leave it for those dear to him to praise him as they knew him: I speak for his effort in behalf of pure blood and pure bodies. The bow of Jonathan turned not back!

Verily it seems as if the nineteenth century as it is passing to its midnight, is carrying with it its representative men; those who gave form to its advancing thought seem to be almost all of them departed. In the world of letters, from Hugo to Holmes, the stalwart ones are gone; the able men of our American politics, whom we have looked to for a half century, are mostly in their graves; of the anti-slavery galaxy only Parker Pillsbury, and one or two others, are still here; and so we may pass around the circle.

In all reformatory matters LUTHER COLBY always spoke manfully. Peace to his name. May he prove to have been but an Elijah, to be speedily followed by an Elisha, endowed by a double portion of the prophetic spirit with ability while exterminating the house of Ahab to save our Israel for a better career.

WILLIAM BERRY,
CO-FOUNDER OF THE BANNER.

MR. BERRY was First Lieutenant of the "Andrew Sharpshooters," attached to the Fifteenth Regiment Massachusetts Volunteers. He was killed at the Battle of Antietam, Md., September 17, 1862, aged 37 years. He was co-worker with Mr. Colby in the establishment of the *Banner of Light*, and continued as its business manager till he joined the service of his country in the Civil War. As a manifesting spirit intelligence he often made his presence known, and wrote through the hand of Mr. Colby frequent messages, that were of much comfort and encouragement to him (C.).

THE AWAKENING.

THE subjoined poem was contributed to *The Banner* by its authoress, MRS. KATE R. STILES, with the explanation that while writing it she felt strongly the inspiration of an intelligence claiming to be spirit LUTHER COLBY. The symbolic picture it conveys is restful indeed to earth-weary hearts.

I slept and as I slept I dreamed,
Or thus unto my sense it seemed,
And in my dream methought I stood
Once more in the familiar wood,
Where oft I wandered as a child.
Again I plucked the blossoms wild
That grew within the wooded dell.
I sensed again their fragrant smell,
And, as I oft had done before,
A handful of these blooms I bore
Unto the old home, standing near,
To glad the heart of mother dear.
Busied about her household cares,
I thought to greet her unawares
With the sweet treasures of the wood ;
I tripped along in happy mood —
Across the meadow, through the lane,
Humming an old familiar strain.
The sun was setting, and its rays
Fell lengthwise, as in olden days,
Across the sanded kitchen floor,
And as I crossed the threshold o'er,
Thinking my mother to surprise,
I met her tender, loving eyes,
And heard her say in sweetest tone,
" Welcome, my darling son, my own."
Oh ! the delightful sense of rest,
As, folded to my mother's breast,
I gazed once more upon her face.
My joy to questioning gave place,

So strange, so very strange, did seem
That which I still did think a dream.
"Tell me," I cried, "my mother dear,
Is it indeed your voice I hear?
Is it indeed your face I see?
Or will this vision fade from me
And carry with it all this joy?
Oh! call me once again your boy,
And tell me that this blessed rest,
This sense of peace within my breast,
Shall not depart, and leave me still
A weary pilgrim, weak and ill."
My mother did to me respond
In accents musical and fond:
"My child, earth's weariness and pain
Will ne'er return to you again;
Henceforth your spirit shall be free,
An heir of Immortality."

While thus she spake I sensed the change —
My vision took a broader range,
And I beheld a concourse great,
Of friends with faces all elate,
Whose words of welcome and of cheer,
Fell like sweet music on my ear.
Some laid fresh blossoms at my feet,
Some with bright banners came to greet,
And all seemed jubilant and glad;
And naught was there to make one sad.
Yet did a sense to pain akin,
Which well I knew came from within,
Sweep o'er my spirit, and I knelt
In deep contrition, for I felt
Myself unworthy of the songs
And greetings of the heavenly throngs.

Then did a spirit o'er me bend,
Saying — "Arise! arise, my friend!
Here all are worthy to receive,
The love that we so freely give;
This concourse vast, that you now see,
Have all been mortals, friend, like thee;

Each understands the pain and strife,
Attendant on an earthly life.
Each in the struggle for life's good,
Has oft, no doubt, misunderstood
The path that led to life's true gain;
All souls mistake, and suffer pain,
And none are wise enough to know
How much of good they really owe
Unto the errors and mistakes
Which every earthly pilgrim makes.
So rise, my friend, and stand erect,
Nor one experience reject;
Some good from each you yet shall see —
Arise, and stand erect and free."

Then from my knees I rose — and, lo!
A garment white and pure as snow
Was by the angel o'er me thrown;
"Wear it," he said, "it is thine own;
Into its warp and woof is spun
The good that you on earth have done.
Each kindly deed, each good intent.
Each purpose of your life, well meant,
Though unfulfilled, is noted here,
And cherished in life's higher sphere."

Oh! what delight within me stirred
As I did listen to the word
Of love and kindly sympathy,
The angel thus bestowed on me.
My spirit now no longer quailed
At thought that I so oft had failed
To do the task to me assigned.
A new resolve possessed my mind:
A resolution that henceforth
My life should prove of greater worth.

Then to my angel guide I said,
"While earthly friends proclaim me dead,
I feel I have but just begun
The course of life, true life, to run."

The angel to my words replied,
"Go back to earth, and seek to guide
The minds of mortals toward the right.
Raise high Truth's Banner, that its light
Full many a pilgrim soul shall see,
And be from error's chains set free."

Then did the angel say, " Farewell,"
Yet still remained the magic spell
That o'er my spirit had been cast,
A spell too full of joy to last.

I lingered for a little time
Among these spirit scenes sublime,
But mortal life enthralled me still,
My earthly longings ruled my will,
And bare me backward to the earth,
Where I had had my mortal birth.

To friends familiar I drew nigh,
Some saw me, and did give reply
Unto my greeting as I came,
To such my coming seemed the same
As erst it seemed in days before,
When I my earthly garment wore.
Others there were to whom I spake
On whom I could no impress make ;
Deaf were they to my strong appeal,
They could not see, nor could they feel
My presence, and I turned away,
Saddened in heart for such as they
Who know not that their loved ones wait,
And call them through affection's gate,
Which death can never, never, close.
Oh! angels, pity, pity those,
"Who hopeless lay their dead away,"
And know not whither they do stray.

To bring the light to such as these,
This be my mission still, God please ;
For this great truth, dear friends, be brave,
For this let the dear *Banner* wave,

Let its pure folds gleam like a star,
To guide earth's pilgrims near and far,
Unto that Truth destined to be
The Savior of humanity.

THE RECEPTION IN SPIRIT-LIFE.

"Ouina," the brilliant, piquant, and yet thoughtful guide of that noted medium, Mrs. Cora L. V. Richmond (whom the spirit denominates "Water-Lily"), contributed to the same journal the appended narration of the welcome extended Mr. Colby in the Higher Life :

How rejoiced we all were, on the spirit side of life, when we saw that at last the noble chief [Colby] was to be set free. He had suffered so much in his body, and his mind had been so often disturbed of late, that we knew the transition would bring great release.

Little do mortals know (or realize if they know) what it is to be enfranchised from the limitations of time and sense.

We had all watched over and tried to relieve his sufferings — I mean "Tululu" (Mrs. Fannie Conant), Vashti, Dr. Pike, the Indian "medicine men," Dr. Rush, and all of the Colby-chief's " children " (the spirit-messengers whom he had adopted as his own), when the Willis chief (Fred. L. H. Willis, who was with him much during the last days) was trying to help and soothe him.

We knew how he would be missed ; but there is always a lessening of the seeming importance of human places, and even duties, under the great stress and urgency of the mighty angel who comes to disenthrall.

He alone, of whom this is written, knows his own inner preparation for this yielding up of the strong fortress in earth-life, in which he had fought the battle for truth from the ramparts of his own integrity, strengthened ever by the unseen, yet palpable ones, who loved him because of his devotion to the truth of Spiritualism.

With a strong nature, engaged in a work in earth-life that is paramount, and accustomed for twoscore years to wield the instrument more mighty than the sword in a cause most sacred, it is not strange if at the gateway of the Change called Beautiful there was a struggle, like that of the meeting and hesitation, of the incoming and outgoing tides, the ebbing and flowing of the life-forces of an impulsive, turbulent, impetuous, child-like, generous, loving and noble heart.

But it came, the Great Supreme, and he was free and aware.

Oh! how I wish you could know — you, dear heart, who may be reading this with eyes dimmed with tears of sorrow, blind, earthly, but tender, human sorrow — what this release really is. Happily, perhaps, human beings dread and shrink from for themselves, and mourn when it comes to others, the one Supreme Benefaction of existence; otherwise earth could not retain them.

Now it had come! He wants me here to say that he never for one instant lost consciousness — either of where he was in bodily form, of what was transpiring in the room with the house of clay, or of what was passing in his own experience. Just as he was when the kind friends in earth-form stood around, so he was, as far as consciousness was concerned, when he recognized *the added company into which he was admitted by added perception.*

That which transpired before us all, and of which he was the most conscious, was truly remarkable: there was an instantaneous *sloughing off* of every pain, care, vexation, weakness, trouble; I never saw a spirit that had suffered so much from these afflictions in the body, so absolutely and instantaneously freed. His spirit *sprang* into his new existence as an acrobat might leap from a prison of paper, or a giant, aroused, might spring from gyves of straw. The vigor, fervor, faith in humanity, hopes of youth, *all* came forth, illumining and transfiguring him instantly! The exclamation was like a prayer of thankfulness that escaped from him, "I feel as young as I did fifty years ago!" What is thanksgiving but the grateful recognition of blessings?

"Tululu" was first to meet him in special recognition; then one by one he perceived his friends and guides, according to their *spiritual* nearness. We wreathed for him those priceless flowers from our home, of which he had fashioned such an abundance; flowers of the kind deeds; acts of benevolence unseen of mortals; true generosity in loving and giving. Ah! how his spirit humbly and as a child received this tender ministration. Through whatever scenes with friends of childhood days, guided by mother love and paternal joy; through whatever reunion of sacred friendships, unsullied, undimmed by time; through the meeting and mingling with those who were *his own*, we may not follow: Spirits who in outward life have been as true and unswerving as was he to his convictions, find their own without any intervening shadow. . . .

Those who have aided him in spreading the gospel of Spiritualism, who have watched and guarded the unfurling of *The Banner* from week to week; those who have prompted, led, checked him (when needed) during those years of service for truth, have no need to make room or place for him in their counsels. HE IS ONE OF THEM!

VALE!

THIS brief compendium of historic record, personal memory and loving tribute is done! Of the imperfections of the work — judged from the standpoint of those who have abundant leisure, and quiet conditions for reflective thought — its author is painfully aware; but it has been necessarily prepared during such hours of leisure as were available in the evening and on the Sabbath — his many and pressing duties as editor of the *Banner of Light* being held by him as sacredly demanding the entire working hours of the week for their discharge.

As the Jews repaired the walls of Jerusalem, when return-ing from captivity, with the alternate use of the sword of de-fence and the trowel·of upraising, so these pages have grown till they meet the perusal of the public ; from his readers the author asks a kindly remembrance of this fact.   He feels as one who " plasters his swallow's nest upon an awful past," yet while its Alpine-glow remains — and cheered by the knowledge that the Spiritual Revelation brings — he would say in con-clusion in the words of another :

> " The presence of that companion,
>   Though we never may see again,
> Shall spread deep roots like the banyan
>   And its perfume shall remain.

> " O friends, we are blundering blindly,
>   Like men in a mist of tears —
> *That presence so true and kindly*
>   *We shall meet in coming years !*

> .   .   .   .

> " So, close up the ranks, my brothers
>   And with hearts too high to fail
> Let us say ' Farewell ' — while the others
>   On the brighter side cry *'All Hail !'* "